THE PROPHET
OF
YONWOOD

The BOOKS of EMBER

THE CITY OF EMBER
THE PEOPLE OF SPARKS
THE PROPHET OF YONWOOD

THE PROPHET
OF
YONWOOD

Jeanne DuPrau

RANDOM HOUSE 🏠 NEW YORK

This is a work of fiction. Names, characters, places, and incidents either are
the product of the author's imagination or are used fictitiously. Any resemblance to
actual persons, living or dead, events, or locales is entirely coincidental.

THE PROPHET

OF

YONWOOD

The Vision

On a warm July afternoon in the town of Yonwood, North Carolina, a woman named Althea Tower went out to her backyard to fill the bird feeder. She opened her sack of sunflower seeds, lifted the bird feeder's lid—and that was when, without warning, the vision assailed her.

It was like a waking dream. The trees and grass and birds faded away, and in their place she saw blinding flashes of light so searingly bright she staggered backward, dropped her sack of birdseed, and fell to the ground. Billows of fire rose around her, and a hot wind roared. She felt herself flung high into the sky, and from there she looked down on a dreadful scene. The whole earth boiled with flames and black smoke. The noise was terrible—a howling and crashing and crackling—and finally, when the firestorm subsided, there came a silence that was more terrible still.

When the vision finally faded, it left Althea stunned. She lay on the ground, unable to move, with her mind all jumbled and birds pecking at the spilled birdseed around her. She might have lain there for hours if Mrs. Brenda Beeson had not happened to come by a few minutes later to bring her a basket of strawberries.

Seeing Althea on the ground, Mrs. Beeson rushed forward. She bent over her friend and spoke to her, but Althea only moaned. So Mrs. Beeson used her cell phone to call for help. Within minutes, four of her best friends—the doctor, the police chief, the town mayor, and the minister of the church—had all arrived. The doctor squatted beside Althea and spoke slowly and loudly. "Can you tell us what's wrong?" he said. "What is it?"

Althea shivered. Her lips twisted as she tried to speak. Everyone leaned in to hear.

"It's God," she whispered. "God. I saw . . . I saw . . ." She trailed off.

"Merciful heavens," said Brenda Beeson. "She's had a vision."

Of course they didn't know at first what her vision had been. They thought maybe she'd seen God. But why would that frighten her so? Why would she be muttering about fire and smoke and disaster?

Days went by, and Althea didn't get better. She lay

on her bed hardly moving, staring into the air and mumbling. Then, exactly a week later, a clue to the mystery came. The president of the United States announced that talks with the Phalanx Nations had reached a crisis. Their leaders would not give in on any of their demands, and the leaders of the United States would not give in on theirs. Unless some sort of agreement could be reached, the president said, it might be necessary to go to war.

Brenda Beeson made the connection right away: War! That must be what Althea Tower had seen. Mrs. Beeson called her friends, they told their friends, the newspaper wrote it up, and soon the whole town knew: Althea Tower had seen the future, and it was terrible.

All over Yonwood, people gathered in frightened clusters to talk. Could it be true? The more they thought about it, the more it seemed it could be. Althea had always been a quiet, sensible person, not the sort to make things up. And these were strange times, what with conflicts and terrorists and talk of the end of the world—just the kind of times when visions and miracles were likely to happen.

Brenda Beeson formed a committee to take care of Althea and pay attention to anything else she might say. People wrote letters to the newspaper about her and left flowers and ribbons and handwritten notes in front of her house. The minister spoke of her in church.

After a few weeks, nearly everyone was calling her the Prophet.

CHAPTER 1

The Inheritance

Nickie Randolph's first sight of the town of Yonwood was a white steeple rising out of the pine forest that covered the mountainside. She leaned forward, gazing through the windshield of the car. "Is that it?"

Her aunt Crystal, who was driving, put one hand up to shield her eyes from the rays of the setting sun. "That's it," she said.

"My new home," said Nickie.

"You have to get that notion out of your mind," said Crystal. "It's not going to happen."

I'm going to *make* it happen, thought Nickie, though she didn't say it out loud. Crystal's mood was already bad enough. "How long till we get there?" she asked.

"We'll be there in twenty minutes, if nothing else gets in our way."

A lot had gotten in their way so far. The Streakline

train was closed down because of the Crisis, so they'd had to drive. They'd been on the road for seven hours, though the trip from Philadelphia should have taken no more than five. But long lines at gas stations, detours around pot-holed or snow-covered stretches of highway, and military roadblocks had slowed them down. Crystal didn't like delays. She was a fast-moving, efficient person, and when her way was blocked, she became very tense and spoke with her lips in two hard lines.

They came to the Yonwood exit, and Crystal turned off the highway onto a road that wound uphill. Here the trees grew thick on either side, and so tall that their bare branches met overhead, making a canopy of sticks. Drops of rain began to spatter the car's wind-shield.

After a while, they came to a sign that said, "Yonwood. Pop. 2,460." The trees thinned out, and the rain fell harder. They passed a few storage sheds, a collapsing barn, and a lumberyard. After that, hous-es began to appear on the side of the road—small, tired-looking wooden houses, their roofs dripping. Many of them had rockers or couches on the front porch, where people would no doubt be sitting if it weren't the dead of winter.

From a small brick shelter at the side of the road, a policeman stepped out holding a red stop sign. He held it up and waved it at them. Crystal slowed down, stopped, and opened her window. The policeman bent down. He had on a rain jacket with the hood up, and rain dripped off the hood and onto his nose. "Hello, ma'am," he said. "Are you a resident?"

"No," said Crystal. "Is that a problem?"

"Just doing a routine entry check, ma'am," the man said. "Part of our safety program. Had some evidence lately of possible terrorist activity in the woods. Your purpose here?"

"My grandfather has died," Crystal said. "My sister and I have inherited his house. I've come to fix the house up and sell it."

The man glanced at Nickie. "This is your sister?"

"This is my niece," said Crystal. "My sister's daughter."

"And your grandfather's name?" said the man.

"Arthur Green," said Crystal.

"Ah, yes," the policeman said. "A fine gentleman." He smiled. "You be careful while you're here, now. We've had reports indicating there may be agents of the Phalanx Nations traveling alone or in small groups in parts of the area. Have you been spoken to by any suspicious strangers?"

"No," said Crystal. "Just you. You seem very suspicious."

"Ha ha," said the man, not really laughing. "All

right, ma'am," he went on. "You may go. Sorry for the delay, but as you know there's a crisis. We're taking every precaution."

He stepped away, and they drove on.

"Terrorists even *here*?" Nickie said.

"It's nonsense," said Crystal. "Why would a terrorist be wandering around in the woods? Pay no attention."

Nickie was so tired of the Crisis. It had been going on now for months. On TV and the radio, it was all you ever heard about: how Our Side and Their Side had come almost, but not quite, to the point of declaring all-out war. In the last week or so, the radio had started broadcasting frightening instructions every hour: "In the event of a declaration of war or a large-scale terrorist attack, cities will be evacuated in an orderly fashion. . . . Residents will be directed to safe locations. . . . Citizens should remain calm. . . ."

It seemed to Nickie that everything in the world had gone wrong—including her own family. Eight months ago, her father had left on a government job. He couldn't tell them where he was going or what he was supposed to do, and he warned that he might not be able to get in touch with them very often. This turned out to be true. She and her mother had had exactly one postcard from him. The postmark had been smudged, so they couldn't tell where the card came from. And the message was no help, either. It said, "Dear Rachel and Nickie, I am working hard, everything is fine, don't worry. I hope you're both doing well. Love, Dad."

But they were not doing well. Nickie's mother missed Nickie's father and couldn't bear not knowing where he was. She worried about losing her job, and so she worked too hard, and so she was always tired and sad. And Nickie hadn't felt happy or safe for a long time. She hated Philadelphia. Something awful seemed always about to happen there. The emergency sirens blasted night and day. Government helicopters circled overhead. In the streets, where trash blew in the wind, dangerous people might be around any corner. And school—a tall, grim building with stinking bathrooms—was just as bad. The books were older than the students, the teachers were too tired to teach, and mean kids prowled the halls. Nickie hated being at school.

But she didn't much like being at home, either, in the big tenth-floor condo where she and her mother lived, with its dusty, unused rooms and its huge plateglass windows that gave a frightening view straight down to the tiny street below. She was home alone too much lately. She was nervous and restless. She'd read half a book and set it down. She'd work on her Amazing Things scrapbook and get bored after pasting in just one picture. She'd gaze through her binoculars at people going by on the street below, which she used to do for hours, but even her endless curiosity seemed to have faded, and she'd turn away after a few minutes. When she was really desperate, she'd turn on the TV, even though there was almost nothing on but news, and the news was always the same: grim government spokesmen, troops in camouflage dashing around in foreign places, and the skeletons of blown-up cars and buses. Sometimes the president would come on, his white hair always brushed perfectly smooth, his neat white beard giving him a look of wisdom. "These are dangerous times," he would say, "but with the help of God we will prevail."

She was lonely at home, with her father gone and her mother always at work, and she was lonely at school, because *both* her best friends had moved— Kate to Washington last year, and Sophy to Florida two months ago. Sometimes, late at night when her mother still wasn't home, Nickie felt like someone in a tiny lifeboat, drifting by itself in a big, dark, dangerous sea.

That was why, as soon as she heard about Greenhaven, her great-grandfather's house in Yonwood, before she'd even seen it, she decided it would be her home. She loved its name; a haven was a safe place, and that's what she wanted. The trouble was, Crystal and her mother wanted to sell it.

"But why can't we sell *this* place instead?" Nickie had said to her mother. "And get out of the horrible city and go live in a beautiful, peaceful place for a change?"

Nickie had actually never been to her great-grandfather's house in Yonwood, except for one time when she was too young to remember. But she'd made up a picture of Yonwood in her mind that she was sure must be close to the truth: it was rather like a Swiss ski village, she decided, where in the winter there would be log fires in fireplaces and big puffy comforters on the beds, and the snow would be pure white, not filthy and gray as it was in the city. In summer, Yonwood would be warm and green, with butterflies. In Yonwood, she would be happy and safe. She desperately wanted to go there.

After days of arguing, she finally convinced her mother to let her at least see the house before it was sold. All right, her mother said. Nickie could take a couple of weeks off school, drive down with Crystal (her mother couldn't leave work), and help her get the place fixed up and put on the market. Nickie agreed, but her real plan was different: somehow she would persuade Crystal to keep the house, not sell it, and she and her mother (and her father, when he came back) would go and live there, and everything would be different, and better.

That was her Goal #1. But since she was sure this was going to be a life-changing trip, she thought she might as well add other goals as well. Altogether, she had set herself three:

1. To keep her great-grandfather's house from being sold so she could live in it with her parents.
2. To fall in love. She was eleven now, and she thought it was time for this. Not to fall in love in a permanent way, just to have the experience of being madly, passionately in love. She knew she was a passionate person. She had a big love inside her, and she needed to give it.
3. To do something helpful for the world. What that would be she had no idea, but the world needed help badly. She would keep her eyes open for an opportunity.

They were driving now up the town's main business street. It was in fact called Main Street—Nickie saw the name on a sign. They passed the church whose steeple Nickie had seen from the highway. In front of it was a two-legged wooden sign that said, in hand-painted letters, "Church of the Fiery Vision." Nickie could tell, though, that the sign used to say something else; the old name of the church had been painted over.

Beyond the church, the shopping district began. Probably it was pretty in summer, Nickie thought, but now, in February, it had a gray and shuttered look, as if the buildings themselves were cold. Some stores were open, and people walked in and out of them, but others looked permanently closed, their windows dark. There was a movie theater, but its ticket booth was boarded up. There was a park, but its swings and picnic tables were wet and empty.

Crystal turned left, drove uphill for a block, and turned right on a street lined with old houses. On one side of this street—it was Cloud Street, its sign said—the ground sloped upward, so that the houses stood up high, at the crest of their lawns. They were huge houses, with columns and wide porches and numerous chimneys. The people in there, Nickie thought, would be sitting beside roaring fires on an evening like this, probably drinking hot chocolate.

"It's this one," said Crystal, drawing in toward the curb.

Nickie gasped. "*This* one?"

"I'm afraid so." Her aunt stopped the car, and Nickie gaped at the house, stunned. Rain poured down, but she opened the window anyway, to get a better look.

It was more of a castle than a house. It loomed over them, immense and massive, three stories high. At one corner was a tower—round, with high windows. The steep slate roof bristled with chimneys. Rain ran down it in sheets, glistening in the last of the daylight.

"You *can't* sell this house," Nickie said. "It's too wonderful."

"It's awful," said her aunt. "You'll see."

A gust of wind dipped the branches of a pine tree that grew close to the house, and Nickie thought she saw a light in a high window.

"Does anyone still live here?" she asked.

"No," said Crystal. "Just the mice and cockroaches."

When Nickie looked up again, the light was gone.

CHAPTER 2

The Third Floor

They put up the hoods of their jackets and dashed through the pelting rain, along the path, up the steps, and across the stone terrace to the wide, wooden door. The Yonwood real estate office had sent Crystal a key; she fitted it into the keyhole, turned it, and pushed the door open.

They stepped into a wide hall. Crystal groped for the light switch, and a light came on, revealing walls hung with gilt-framed paintings of old-fashioned people, such old paintings that they were nearly black. At the end of the hall was a flight of stairs curving up into the darkness.

Through an archway to the left was the dining room, where chairs stood around a long table. Through an archway to the right was the living room. "The front parlor," Crystal said, turning on a lamp. It was a gloomy room: dark red curtains at the windows, floor-length; walls lined halfway up with bookcases, and above the bookcases red fuzzy wallpaper; Persian rugs on the floor, thin as sheets of burlap, patterned in dusty blue and faded red. And beside the window, a long couch with three bed pillows and two blankets neatly folded.

"This must have been where Grandfather spent his last days," Crystal said.

"Who took care of him?" Nickie asked.

"He hired a girl, I believe. For those last few weeks, he wasn't able to cook for himself, and he needed help to get around." Crystal reached out and picked something up from a side table. "Look," she said. "Here he is. Grandfather." It was a silver-framed photograph of a smiling, silver-haired man. "You would have liked him," Crystal said. "He was interested in everything, just like you."

Nickie studied the man in the photograph. He was very old; his skin sagged, but his eyes were lively.

Crystal strode to a window and swept back the curtains. "What I need to do," she said, "is make a list of the valuables." She took a notebook out of her big purse. "I may as well start on it, as long as we're here. I think there might be some first editions among the books."

"I'm going to look around, okay?" said Nickie. "I want to see everything."

Her aunt nodded.

Nickie went back through the dining room and through a swinging door that led to the most ancient kitchen she had ever seen. It had a smell so indescribably repellent that she hurried away down a passage that led behind the front parlor.

There she found two bedrooms, each with a towering four-poster bed of black carved wood and a great black chest of drawers topped with a mirror in a heavy frame. Up on the second floor were four more bedrooms. She pulled open a few drawers, expecting to find them empty. But they were filled with folded clothes and jewelry boxes and hairbrushes and old bottles of dried-up perfume. It looked as if no one had ever cleaned these rooms out after their occupants had gone away or died.

There was a study on the second floor, too, where a computer sat on a desk, and a lot of file folders and papers and books lay scattered around the room. Her great-grandfather must have worked here. He'd been a college professor before he retired, but Nickie wasn't sure what he'd been a professor *of.* Some sort of science.

It was strange, she thought. Until just a few days ago, this house had been lived in continuously for over 150 years. It was never vacant, and it was never sold— her ancestors had always owned it. Children had grown up here. Old people had died. The house had been so full of life for so long that it probably felt like a living thing itself—and now, in its sudden emptiness, knowing its family no longer wanted it, she imagined it must feel frightened and lonely. Well, *I* want you, she thought. I think you're wonderful.

Remembering that there was a third story, Nickie looked for another stairway. She found it behind a door to the left of the big front stairs—these weren't broad and polished but narrow and plain. There was no handrail along the wall.

At the top was a closed door. She opened it to find herself in a hall with two doors on each side. She looked into all the rooms. Two of them were crammed full of stuff: suitcases and boxes and hatboxes, enormous old trunks with leather straps, stacks of papers and portraits in broken frames and mildewed books and paper-wrapped packages and grocery bags stuffed with who knows what, all of it draped in swags of dusty cobwebs.

The third room was a tiny bathroom that hadn't been cleaned for a while.

But the fourth room was wonderful. It was big and airy, with windows on two sides. The tower formed one corner of it, making a circular alcove with windows all around and a wide window seat running beneath them—the perfect place for sitting with a book on a sunny day, or with lamplight over your shoulder on a dark day like this one. Nickie guessed that this room had been a nursery, because old toys were jumbled into cabinets along one wall. A rolled-up rug lay at one end of the room, and by the windows was a rocking chair. At the far end of the room stood an iron bed, neatly made, as if just waiting for her.

This would be her room, she decided. She loved it already.

As she was about to go back into the hall, a sound stopped her. It was a sort of squeak, or cry, cut short as if someone had clapped a hand over the squeaker's mouth. Nickie stood still and listened. At first she heard nothing—just the patter of the rain on the windows. She was about to move on when she heard it again—two squeaks this time, and a bump. It seemed to be coming from the closet.

She froze, suddenly remembering the light she'd seen from the street. What if someone dangerous was hiding in the closet? A burglar surprised in the middle of a burglary? Or a homeless person who'd sneaked into the house? Or even a terrorist? She hesitated.

There was another squeak—very faint, but definitely coming from the closet. In a choked voice, Nickie said, "Who's in there?"

No answer.

Nickie's curiosity took over. This happened to her a lot. Her hunger for finding things out was so strong that it overcame caution and even common sense. So now, although she was afraid, she dashed to the closet, flung open the door, and leapt back.

Inside, pressed up against the rear wall, half hidden by shirts and dresses dangling from hangers, was a tall, thin girl with wide, terrified eyes. Her hands were wrapped around the muzzle of a small, wildly squirming dog.

CHAPTER 3

The Girl in the Closet

Nickie stared. The girl stared back. The dog wriggled in her arms and paddled its hind legs frantically.

"Who are you?" Nickie asked.

The girl hunched up her shoulders and craned her head toward Nickie. She had a long face and thin brown straggly hair. Her front teeth were a little crooked. "Please," she said in a hoarse whisper. "Don't tell that I'm here. Please don't tell." The girl stepped cautiously out of the closet. "I'm not supposed to be here," she said. The dog wrenched its muzzle out of her hands and yelped. She grabbed it again. She was wearing jeans and a limp green sweater. Nickie could see that the girl was older than she was—a teenager.

"But why *are* you here?" said Nickie.

"I took care of the old man," the girl said. She spoke in a trembly whisper. "For the last six months, till he died. But now I don't have nowhere to go, and if they find me, they'll put me in a home. And take him away." She ducked her chin toward the dog. "So I need to stay here till I can figure out what to do next."

"What's your name?" Nickie asked. She spoke in a whisper, too.

"Amanda Stokes," said the girl. "What's yours?"

Nickie told her. "Arthur Green was my great-grandfather," she said. "My family owns this house now."

"Oh, Lord," said Amanda. She had a worried-looking face, as if she'd been worrying all her life. "Are you going to come and live here?"

"Yes," said Nickie firmly. "But not right away."

"So you won't tell that I'm here?"

Nickie considered. Would it be wrong to keep this girl a secret? She didn't want to do anything wrong. But it seemed to her that telling on Amanda would cause more harm than not. What would it matter if she stayed here a few days longer?

"I can live here real quietly," Amanda said. The dog jerked in her arms and tried to yelp. "Even with him. He's pretty quiet, usually."

"What's his name?"

"Otis. I found him a couple days ago out by the dump. I know he doesn't have no owner, because he didn't have a collar and he was real dirty. I washed him in the laundry sink."

Nickie scratched the dog behind his small, pointed ears. He was a light-colored dog, a sort of strawberry blond, with round brown eyes. His fur grew in a way that made his face look like a ragged sunflower.

From somewhere downstairs came Crystal's voice. "Nickie! Where are you?"

Nickie dashed into the hall and shouted down. "Upstairs!"

"Come on down!" called her aunt. "Let's get settled in."

She went back into the bedroom. "Okay," she said. "I won't tell about you, but you have to be really quiet. Stuff some rags under the door—this door and the hall door both. I'll try and keep my aunt from coming up here. If she's going to, I'll try to warn you."

"Oh, thank you," Amanda said. "Thank you a lot. It's just for a couple days. I'm looking for a job, and when I get one I'll find me a place of my own."

Nickie nodded. "Goodbye," she said, and she dashed back down the stairs.

For dinner that night, they had tomato soup from a can Crystal found in a cupboard. They sat at the big dining room table and ate while the rain beat on the windows. On a pad of paper, Crystal started making a list of all the things she'd have to do to get the house ready for sale: *Call cleaning service. Call auction house.*

Call salvage place. Talk to lawyer. Call painters. Call plumbers. It was clear to Nickie that Crystal would be spending a lot of time on the phone.

"Crystal," Nickie said. "I don't see anything so awful about Greenhaven. Why do you say it's awful?"

"It's huge and dark and impossible to clean. The kitchen is unspeakable. The plumbing is ancient. The whole place smells like mice. That's just for a start."

"But it could be repaired, couldn't it?"

"With great effort and expense." Crystal went back to her list. *Schedule open house,* she wrote. She tapped a long red fingernail on the table, thinking.

Crystal wasn't exactly beautiful, but she always wore stylish clothes and fixed herself up—nail polish, earrings, makeup. Her hair was a sort of streaky blondish color that required frequent visits to the beauty salon. She'd been married twice. First there'd been Uncle Brent, and later there'd been Uncle Brandon. Now there was no one, which was probably one reason Crystal was more snappish and impatient than usual.

"Crystal," said Nickie, "if you could live in any kind of house, what kind would it be?"

Crystal looked up. She gazed at Nickie blankly for a second, her mind elsewhere. Then she said, "Well, I can tell you what it *wouldn't* be. It wouldn't be an old pile like Greenhaven. And it wouldn't be a dinky, tacky little apartment like the one I live in now."

"What, then?" said Nickie.

"A gracious house," said Crystal. "Big rooms, big windows, a big garden. And—" She leaned forward and smiled a wry little smile. "A nice big man to live in it with me."

Nickie laughed. "*Another* husband?" she said.

"The first two weren't quite right," said Crystal.

"Would you want to have a dog?"

"A *dog*? Heavens no. Dogs ruin furniture."

"But if a dog just showed up and needed a home, would you keep it?"

"Certainly not. It would go straight to the pound to wait for a happy life with someone else." She spooned up the last of her soup. "Why are you asking about dogs?"

"Just wondering," said Nickie, with a sinking heart. "I like dogs."

After dinner, Crystal went to take a bath and Nickie dashed up to the third floor. She tapped on the door of the nursery, and Amanda, in her pajamas, opened it. Otis stood on his hind legs to greet Nickie, and she hugged and petted him. "Everything okay?" she asked Amanda.

"Yeah," Amanda said. "I'm being real quiet."

"Good," said Nickie. "Because I found out Crystal doesn't like dogs. We have to be extremely careful."

"Okay," said Amanda. "I'll put him under the covers with me tonight."

25

Nickie gave Otis one more pat and hurried back downstairs. For a while, she and Crystal sat in the front parlor and watched the news.

A local announcer was talking. "Several residents in Hickory Cove and Creekside," he said, "have reported signs of unusual activity in nearby wooded areas. A hiker claims to have caught a glimpse, in a remote part of the woods, of a man wearing a white or light tan coat. Residents of the area are advised to be alert to anything out of the ordinary, including unknown persons arriving in town; evidence of tampering with buildings, pipelines, or electrical equipment; and strange behavior of any kind."

Then the president came on. Nickie didn't like listening to him because his voice always sounded too smooth. He said something about the Phalanx Nations and missile deployment and fourteen countries and Level Seven alerts. Crystal frowned. "It gets closer every day," she said.

"What does?"

Crystal just shook her head. "Big trouble," she said.

The president ended with his usual sentence: "Let us pray to God for the safety of our people and the success of our endeavors." Nickie always wondered about this. The idea seemed to be that if you prayed extremely hard—especially if a *lot* of people prayed at once—maybe God would change things. The trouble was, what if your enemy was praying, too? Which prayer would God listen to?

She sighed. "Crystal," she said, "I'm so sick of the Crisis."

"I know," said Crystal. She flicked off the TV. "We all are. But it doesn't help to worry. All we can do is keep our wits about us. Not let fear take over. And try to be good little people and not add to the badness." She smiled at Nickie and stood up. "Tired?"

Nickie nodded.

"Which room would you like to sleep in?" Crystal asked. "You can have first pick."

The room she really wanted was the one on the third floor, but right now it was occupied. So Nickie chose one of the bedrooms on the first floor, and Crystal took the one next to it. They found sheets and blankets in a linen closet and made up the beds, and they unpacked their suitcases and hung their clothes in the closets. Nickie put her nightie on and slid between the sheets of the enormous bed. She thought about Amanda and the little dog, hidden away upstairs. They would be going to bed now, too. It would be nice, she thought, to sleep with a dog curled up next to you.

The bed's black posts rose toward the ceiling; in the darkness, they looked like two thin soldiers standing guard. Nickie wondered who this room had belonged to in years past. Who else had lain here looking at those posts, and at the violet-flowered wallpaper, and the stains on the ceiling? She wished she could know about their lives—not just her grandfather's but all the lives of this house, all those ancestors she'd never known.

This is how Nickie was: she wanted to know about everybody and everything—not just encyclopedia-type information, but ordinary things like what people did at their jobs and what their houses looked like inside and what they talked about. When she passed two or three people walking together on the street, she always hoped to catch an intriguing bit of conversation, like "I found her lying there dead!" Or ". . . and he left that very day without telling a soul and was never seen again!" But almost always, all she heard were the dull, connecting bits of the conversation, things like "And so I said to her . . ." and "Yeah, I think so, too," and "So it's really kind of like . . ." And by the time they said whatever came next, they were out of earshot.

She also wanted to know about things that weren't so ordinary, strange *extra*ordinary things like, Were there people on other planets? Was ESP real? Were there still places on Earth where no one had ever been? Were there animals that no one had yet discovered? In a magazine, she had come across a photograph of a dust mite taken with an electron microscope. A dust mite was much too small to see with the naked eye, but when you took its picture and magnified it many times, you could see that it was as complicated and weird as a monster in a science-fiction movie, with fangs and feelers and bristles.

When Nickie saw this picture, she suddenly understood that a whole other world existed right alongside the world of things she could see. In the dust under the furniture, in between the strands of the carpet, even crawling on her very own skin and inside her guts were creatures of unbelievable strangeness. She loved knowing this. She took the dust mite picture with her everywhere she went.

Now she listened to the rain pattering steadily at the windows and closed her eyes. She thought about the spirits of all the people who had lived here. Maybe they were still hovering around, wondering who was coming next. It's going to be me, she told them silently. *I'm* going to live here. And this reminded her of something she'd forgotten to do. She sat up and turned the light back on. In the drawer of the bedside table, she rummaged around until she found a stubby pencil and a scrap of paper. On the paper she wrote:

1. Keep Greenhaven.
2. Fall in love.
3. Help the world.

Her three goals. She was determined to accomplish them all.

CHAPTER 4

Break-In

Sometime in the middle of that night, as the rain fell and Nickie slept, someone—or something—came out of the forest above the town. The night was dark and moonless, and whoever it was came so quietly that no one heard him. Wayne Hollister, who ran the Black Oak Inn at the north end of town, glanced out the window when he got up to go to the bathroom around 2:00 a.m., and he was pretty sure he saw something moving on the road, but he didn't have his glasses on, so he couldn't tell what it was. Maybe a man in a raincoat.

Early the next morning—it was a Friday—a boy named Grover Persons was walking up the alley in back of the Cozy Corner Café, hunting for a particular kind of wildlife on his way to school, when he noticed that the glass window next to the café's back door was broken. He stopped to investigate. He could see that the window must have been punched in from the outside. A few fragments lay on the ground below the window, but most of the glass was inside, scattered across the restaurant's kitchen counter. Some jagged shards remained in the window frame, and something else was there, too: it looked like a white dish towel snagged on the broken glass. On the towel was a dark stain. Grover peered at it. It looked like blood.

He went around to the front of the restaurant, where Andy Hart, the manager, was just opening up.

"Andy," said Grover, "someone broke your back window last night."

Andy stood stock-still and gaped at him for a second. Sunlight, which shone through gaps in the left-over rain clouds, flashed on his glasses and lit up his high, shiny forehead. Then he charged around to the back, with Grover behind him. When he saw the broken window and the stained cloth, he let out a shriek that brought people running from all around. In minutes, the entire four-man police force and ten or twelve other people had gathered behind the Cozy Corner. They stared at the broken window, which looked like a great snaggle-toothed mouth with a bloody tongue hanging out the bottom.

"Stay back," said Chief of Police Ralph Gurney. "Don't touch anything. This is a crime scene."

People moved back. Grover could hear them murmuring to each other in worried voices.

"Andy, you in there?" called Officer Gurney through the window. "What's been taken?"

From inside, Andy called, "Nothing much. It looks like just a package of chicken."

"So," said Officer Gurney. "This must be either a prank or a threat."

Again came the uneasy murmurs from the crowd.

At another time, this broken window might have seemed like a minor incident. After all, no one was hurt; not much was stolen. But people were already on edge. It had been more than six months since Althea Tower had had her terrible vision, and every day that vision seemed closer to coming true. Just last night, the Phalanx Nations had announced that they had missiles deployed in fourteen countries. The United States had replied by raising the alert level to Seven. Everyone knew that terrorists were all over the place. It seemed that the evils of the world were coming far too close for comfort.

Officer Gurney ran a strip of yellow tape around the back area of the café, roping it off so no one could disturb the site. Then he scanned the crowd. His eyes lit on a comfortably plump woman wearing a red down jacket that made her look even plumper. She had a short brownish-blond ponytail that stuck out through a hole in her red baseball hat.

"Brenda," said Officer Gurney. "What do you think?"

Grover was in danger of being late for school by this time. He'd already been late twice this month. If he was late again, he might get a note sent home to his parents. But he had to risk it. This was too interesting to miss.

The woman stepped forward. Grover knew her, of course; everyone did. Mrs. Brenda Beeson was the one who had figured out the Prophet's mumbled words and explained what they meant. She and her committee—the Reverend Loomis, Mayor Orville Milton, Police Chief Ralph Gurney, and a few others— were the most important people in the town.

Officer Gurney raised the yellow tape so Mrs. Beeson could duck under it. She stood before the window a long time, her back to the crowd, while everyone waited to see what she would say. Clouds sailed slowly across the sun, turning everything dark and light and dark again.

To Grover, it seemed like ages they all stood there, holding their breath. He resigned himself to being late for school and started thinking up creative excuses. The front door of his house had stuck and he couldn't get it open? His father needed him to help fish drowned rats out of flooded basements? His knee had popped out of joint and stayed out for half an hour?

Finally Mrs. Beeson turned to face them. "Well, it just goes to show," she said. "We never *used* to have people breaking windows and stealing things. For all our hard work, we've *still* got bad eggs among us." She gave an exasperated sigh, and her breath made a puff of fog in the chilly air. "If this is someone's idea of fun, that person should be very, very ashamed of himself. This is no time for wild, stupid behavior."

"It's probably kids," said a man standing near Grover. Why did people always blame kids for things like this? As far as Grover could tell, grown-ups caused a lot more trouble in the world than kids.

"On the other hand," said Mrs. Beeson, "it could be a threat, or a warning. We've heard the reports about someone wandering around in the hills." She glanced back at the bloody rag hanging in the window. "It might even be a message of some sort. It looks to me like that stain could be a letter, maybe an *S*, or an *R*."

Grover squinted at the stain on the cloth. To him it looked more like an *A*, or maybe even just a random blotch.

"It might be a *B*," said someone standing near him.

"Or an *H*," said someone else.

Mrs. Beeson nodded. "Could be," she said. "The *S* could stand for *sin*. Or if it's an *R* it could stand for *ruin*. If you'll let me have that piece of cloth, Ralph, I'll show it to Althea and see if she has anything to say about it."

Just then Wayne Hollister happened to pass by, saw the crowd, and chimed in about what he'd seen in the night. His story frightened people even more than the blood and the broken glass. All around him, Grover heard them murmuring: Someone's out there. He's given us a warning. What does he mean to do? He's trying to scare us. One woman began to cry. Hoyt McCoy, as usual, said that Brenda Beeson should not pronounce upon things until she was in full possession of the facts, which she was not, and that to him the blotches of blood looked more like a soupspoon than an *R*. Several people told him angrily to be quiet.

But Grover had lost interest now that he'd heard Mrs. Beeson's verdict. If he ran really fast, he might not be late after all. He took off.

When he got to school, he told the first person he saw about the break-in, and then he told the next person, and pretty soon kids were crowding up around him. His friend Martin handed him a piece of paper and told him to draw the blood blot on it, exactly the way it was.

"I can't remember it *exactly*," he said. "But it was more or less like this." He drew a gloppy string of blotches.

"That's supposed to look like a letter?" Martin frowned, peering at Grover's drawing through his thick-framed glasses.

"Well, I'm not drawing it perfect. Maybe it was

more like this." He drew a different blob. "That's not it, either." He laughed.

But Martin frowned again. "Do it right," he said. "I don't appreciate the way you're clowning around."

Grover drew it again, as well as he could remember.

"And she said it was an *S* or an *R*?" Martin wanted to know.

"She wasn't sure which," said Grover.

"And what did she say it stood for?" someone asked.

He told them, and he answered a lot of other questions, too, showing how Officer Gurney had strung the yellow tape, and repeating what Mrs. Beeson had said, and imitating, with a few high-pitched screams thrown in, the sobs of the woman who'd been so frightened. He imitated Hoyt McCoy, too, copying his gloomy look so well that everyone laughed. "Hoyt McCoy said it looked like a soupspoon," he said.

"Yeah," said Martin, "but Hoyt McCoy is a weirdo."

"Maybe so," said Grover, "but Mrs. Beeson doesn't know everything."

"Grover!" said Martin. His voice rose, and his face turned almost the same red as his hair. "*She* took the Prophet's vision seriously, even if *you* didn't."

The bell rang. Grover was late after all, and so was

everyone who'd been listening to him. "Gotta go," he said.

Martin scowled at him. "This will be my first late mark of the whole year," he said.

"It's not *my* fault," said Grover. "You didn't have to stand around talking to me."

But Martin just turned away. He'd changed, thought Grover as he hurried toward his classroom. He used to be nicer than he was now.

CHAPTER 5

The Fiery Vision

That morning, Crystal poked around in the kitchen cupboards and found just about nothing fit to eat. "Would you feel like walking downtown and getting us a few groceries?" she asked Nickie. "I'll start cleaning up this foul kitchen."

So Nickie put on her jacket and went downhill two blocks to Main Street, thinking how nice it was to be out by herself, as she couldn't safely be in the city. The stores were just opening. It was cold, but the sun came out sometimes from between the clouds, and the town looked washed clean. Quite a few people were already out. She noticed that nearly all of them held cell phones to their ears as they walked. Of course she was used to seeing cell phones in the city; there, half the people you passed were jabbering away. But here people weren't *talking* into their phones; they were just listening. It was odd.

She passed a small restaurant called the Cozy Corner Café, where several people were standing outside, talking in excited voices, and a police car was just pulling away. Something must have happened there—maybe a customer had taken sick.

She passed a drugstore, a bakery, and a shoe store. She passed a closed-up movie theater, where a sign stuck over the ticket window said, "Pray instead!" In the window of a clothing store, she saw a display of white T-shirts that said, "Don't Do It!" in big red letters on the front, and after that she kept noticing people on the street wearing these T-shirts. Don't do what? she wondered.

As she passed an alley between a hardware store and a computer repair shop, she heard a strange sound. It was a kind of hum with a rhythm to it— *MMMM-mmmm-MMMM-mmmm*—a sound that a machine might make. She stopped and looked around, but she couldn't see where it was coming from. She could tell that other people on the sidewalk noticed the sound, too. They frowned, but they didn't seem puzzled by it, just annoyed, or maybe a little frightened— a few of them started walking faster, as if to get away. The sound faded after a moment. Nickie decided it must be some gadget in the computer shop.

Farther on, she found the Yonwood Market, and there she bought some bread, milk, eggs, and powdered cocoa. She bought a small box of dog biscuits, too, and tucked this under her jacket.

Nickie was just turning off Main Street on the way back to Greenhaven when, from high overhead, there came a distant roar that quickly rose to a piercing scream, and five fighter jets streaked across the sky. Jets came often these days; they scared her. She stopped walking, set down the bag of groceries, and put her hands over her ears until the jets were gone.

Then she felt someone touch her shoulder. She looked up to see an elderly woman standing over her. "It might be starting," the woman said in a shaky voice. "It might be starting right now—you never know—but it's best not to be scared if you can help it. You need to have faith; that's what I say. We'll be all right here because of what we're doing, as long as we have faith, that's the main thing." The spidery hand patted Nickie's shoulder. "So don't worry, little girl, and remember to pray, and . . ." The woman glanced upward. "We'll be all right, because . . ." She trailed off and tottered away, leaving Nickie feeling the opposite of reassured. Maybe people here were just as scared as they were in the city. That made her heart sink a little. But on the other hand, the woman had said, "We'll be all right." It was confusing.

Once she got back to Greenhaven, though, she forgot about it. She hid the dog biscuits in her bedroom and then went into the kitchen, where Crystal made hot chocolate for them. They sat at the huge, elegant dining room table. Crystal got out her to-do list.

"This room is so . . . majestic," Nickie said. She had decided to point out good things about Greenhaven as often as she could, to change Crystal's mind about selling it.

"I suppose so," said Crystal, glancing up. "Certainly this table is very fine. It should fetch a good price." She went back to her list. "I'll start by talking to the real estate agent," she said. "Then I'll go make arrangements at the auction house and find a cleaning service. I should be back by noon."

"I'll stay here," said Nickie. "I can start going through stuff."

"You'll be all right? You won't fall down the stairs or lean out high windows?"

"Of course I won't," said Nickie. "I'll just take stuff out of cupboards and boxes and look at it. I'll separate it into Stuff to Keep and Stuff to Throw Away."

"Throw Away will be the big pile," Crystal said.

When Crystal had gone, Nickie fetched the dog biscuits and dashed up the stairs. "Amanda!" she called. "It's me!" She heard barking when she came to the door at the top. When she opened it, she saw Otis rocketing toward her. He skidded to a stop in front of her and rose to his hind feet, stretching his front paws up as if he wanted to pat her face. She knelt down and scratched his ears. "Hi, Otis," she said. "You sure are cute."

Amanda came out into the hall. She was still in her bathrobe.

"I heard Otis barking when I came up the stairs," Nickie said. "I don't see how we can keep him a secret if he barks. Crystal will hear him."

"Oh, Lord," said Amanda. "Maybe I could get him a muzzle."

"That seems kind of cruel," Nickie said. "There must be a better way."

Nickie went into the nursery room and looked around. The long tube of rolled-up rug gave her an idea. "We could soundproof this room," she said. "I'm sure we could."

They spent the next two hours doing it. They unrolled the big rug. They found small rugs in other rooms, brought them up to the nursery, and spread them out to cover the entire floor. From bathrooms and linen closets they brought towels and blankets, which they hung over the windows and the door with thumbtacks. Every now and then Nickie would go downstairs, Amanda would get Otis to bark, and Nickie would listen hard. Finally, after four tries, Nickie couldn't hear a thing.

"It works!" she said when she came back up. She

surveyed what they'd done. It was more than a sound-proof room: it was also a strange and beautiful room, almost like the inside of a tent, with its carpeted floor and walls hung with blankets. It glowed with patterns and colors—faded blue and faded red on the floor, rose and lavender, pale green and gold on the walls. The light was dim now, because they'd covered some of the windows, so they brought up a lamp with a parchment shade from one of the rooms below, and more cushions for the window seat, and another rocking chair.

"If only we could make a fire in the fireplace," Nickie said, "this would be the coziest room in the world."

"It's real nice," Amanda agreed. "Otis might chew these rugs, though."

"I'll buy him some toys," Nickie said. "You can teach him to chew those instead." She bent down and rumpled Otis's ears. "Now," she said, "I'm going to start looking through stuff."

"Looking through what?"

"Everything in the house. I want to see it all," Nickie said. "Have you noticed any scrapbooks while you've been here? Or diaries, or photograph albums?"

Amanda pondered. "Maybe in the front parlor cabinet," she said.

So Nickie went downstairs, filled a box with stuff

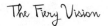

she found in the parlor cabinets, and took it back up to the nursery. She and Amanda sat on the window seat beneath a lamp and looked through it. A great deal of it was boring: old packs of bent playing cards, a calendar from 1973, a photo album containing eighteen faded photos, every one of them of a black cocker spaniel. But there were also some old letters, some *National Geographic* magazines, and quite a few albums with pictures of people. Jammed way in the back, she found three very old-looking cards with black borders. They were from different people, but all of them were dated 1918, and all of them, in old-fashioned handwriting, said more or less the same thing: "We send heartfelt condolences for your tragic loss." What was the tragic loss? she wondered. None of the cards said.

"Hey, I thought of something else you'd probably want to look at," Amanda said. "I'll go get it."

She went downstairs and came back up in a minute with a little brown notebook. "The old man wrote in this sometimes when I was taking care of him," she said, handing it to Nickie.

Nickie opened the notebook. Her great-grandfather's name was written inside the front cover: Arthur Green. She leafed through it. It looked more like a series of jottings than a real journal. He'd made the first entry at the beginning of December, just a couple of months ago. It said:

12/7 Some odd experiences lately. Might be my failing mind, but might not. Will note them down here.

Interesting, Nickie thought. She put the notebook in the Stuff to Keep pile. She'd look at it later.

Otis, in the meantime, chewed quietly on a chair leg. By the time they realized it, he had made some rather deep tooth marks. Fortunately they were on the back leg of the chair and didn't show too much.

Amanda took one of the *National Geographic* magazines and leafed through it. "Oh, Lord, look at this," she said. She held out the magazine, open to a picture of a volcano erupting, with flames and billows of black smoke. "This is kind of like what the Prophet saw."

"Who?"

"The Prophet!" said Amanda. "Althea Tower! You haven't heard of her? She's famous! Everybody in this whole town follows her! Or just about everybody."

"Why do you call her the Prophet?"

"Because she is one," said Amanda. She propped her elbows on her knees and leaned forward. She spoke in the hushed voice people use for imparting awesome information. "She saw the future in a vision."

"What did she see?" asked Nickie.

"Well, she couldn't exactly tell, because it was so

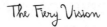

awful it made her sick. She could only give hints. Like she said 'fire' a lot, and 'explosions.' It musta looked sort of like this"—Amanda tapped her finger on the volcano picture—"except all over the world. Anyway, she took to her bed and she's been there ever since."

"That's amazing," said Nickie. "But I don't understand. What did it mean? Was it like a bad dream?"

"It wasn't a *dream*," Amanda said scornfully. "It was the *future*. It was a warning. Mrs. Beeson figured that out."

"Who's Mrs. Beeson?" Nickie asked.

"This lady who lives down the street from here. She's a real sweet, smart lady, used to be the school principal. She has a dog named Sausage; you'll probably see her walking it sometimes." She leaned forward again. "So anyway," she said, "what happened is, people have strayed from God's way, so that's why everything is so awful and heading for doom. But God wants to save us, so he gave the vision to Althea. If we do right, we'll be saved, and what she seen in her vision won't happen. At least not to *us*."

"So what are we supposed to do?" Nickie asked.

"Everything the Prophet says, because it's God's orders coming through her. She tells us what things to give up."

"Give up?"

"Yeah. Like one thing she says a lot is 'No sinnies,' which Mrs. Beeson says means 'No sinners.' We have to be real careful to be good. Also she says 'No singing,' so we don't listen to the pop radio anymore, or CDs, or movies that have singing. And on TV we only watch the news." Otis wandered over, and Amanda reached out absently to scratch him.

"But why?"

"It's to practice not being selfish. So you have more love to give to God." Amanda sat back, looked at Nickie in a satisfied way, and closed the *National Geographic* with a slap.

Nickie pondered. It was true that giving things up was something that holy people often did. She knew that some monks and priests gave up marriage. Some of them even gave up talking and lived their lives in silence. In other countries, there were holy people who gave up comfortable beds and slept on nails. People like these, she supposed, were totally devoted to God. Maybe she herself should give something up, just to see how it felt.

"Did *you* give anything up?" she asked Amanda.

"I did," Amanda said. "I gave up romance books. Mrs. Beeson says they're a waste of time anyway, so it was good to give them up."

"Hmmm," said Nickie. This was just the sort of thing that fired her imagination. It was like something out of a book, the kind of book where dark forces are trying to take over the universe and only a few valiant people know how to defeat them and are brave

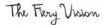

enough to do it. She thought of her Goal #3—to do something helpful for the world. Maybe giving things up was one way to do it. She wanted to ask more questions, but Amanda set down the *National Geographic* at that point and stood up.

"I'm gonna get me a piece of toast," she said. "Want to come?"

Nickie nodded. They left Otis closed into his room and went downstairs. In the kitchen, Amanda sliced the bread, and Nickie, thinking about how interesting it would be to have visions and what she would do if she had one, put on the teakettle for more hot chocolate. But just as Amanda was getting the peanut butter out of the cupboard, though they hadn't heard a single footstep or a knock, a face appeared at the window of the back door. A voice cried, "Hello-o!" in a yoo-hoo sort of way, and before they could move, the door opened.

CHAPTER 6

Mrs. Beeson's Idea

"Excuse me, dears," said the woman at Greenhaven's back door. "I thought I'd stop by and say hello." She stepped inside. "I'm Brenda Beeson," she said.

Nickie stared. Brenda Beeson, the friend of the Prophet! But she didn't look especially holy. She was a middle-aged woman, not exactly fat, but sort of pillowy, with round rosy cheeks. She had on a quilted red jacket, and her blue eyes gleamed out from beneath the visor of a red baseball cap. She looked like a mixture of a grandmother and a soccer coach, Nickie thought.

"You must be Professor Green's granddaughter," Mrs. Beeson said.

"Great-granddaughter," said Nickie. She told Mrs. Beeson her name.

"Nickie?" said Mrs. Beeson. "Short for Nicole?"

"Yes." Nickie never used her real name, Nicole. It was a pretty name, she thought, but it felt *too* pretty for her, since she was rather stocky and had a round chin, a short nose, and straight, unstylish brown hair. She considered herself a smart person with a good imagination but sort of ordinary-looking, and so Nickie felt like a better name.

"Pleased to meet you," said Mrs. Beeson. "I'm your neighbor. I live three houses down, across the street." She took off her cap and stuffed it in her pocket, and Nickie saw that she had caramel-colored hair pulled back in a jaunty ponytail, and she wore little bobbly earrings. Mrs. Beeson turned her gaze on Amanda. "I didn't expect to see *you* here, dear," she said.

Amanda had backed up against the sink. She had a piece of bread in one hand and a jar of peanut butter in the other, and she looked scared.

"Why haven't you left," said Mrs. Beeson, "now that Professor Green has passed?"

"I'm about to go," said Amanda. "Soon as I find a place."

"Find a place? You have no family to go to?"

Amanda just shook her head.

"No parents?"

"My mom died," Amanda said. "My dad took off."

"No one else?"

"Just my cousin LouAnn," Amanda said miserably. "I don't like her."

"Well, dear, this won't do at all," said Mrs. Beeson. She unzipped her jacket with one quick pull and sat down at the kitchen table, ready to handle Amanda's future. Nickie noticed a round blue button pinned to her sweater. The picture on it looked like a little building. "I'm sure I can help," Mrs. Beeson said. "I have several friends in social work. I'll contact them right away. They'll be able to place you in a home." She pulled a little phone out of her pocket—a cell phone, Nickie guessed, though it had a different shape from the ones she was used to.

Amanda took a step forward. Terror was written on her face. She dropped the piece of bread and clunked down the peanut butter jar and raised her hands like stop signs in the direction of Mrs. Beeson. "I don't want to go to any home," she said. "I'm seventeen, I can get a job, I can find—"

"Nonsense," said Mrs. Beeson kindly. "Everyone needs a home." She paused, her mouth half open. An idea seemed to be forming behind her eyes. Her eyebrows rose. "In fact," she said, "I know someone who needs a helper right now. A dear friend of mine."

"What kind of helper?" asked Amanda suspiciously.

"A household helper," Mrs. Beeson said. "A live-in helper."

"I don't know," said Amanda. She hunched up her shoulders and scowled at the floor.

"The friend I am speaking of," said Mrs. Beeson with a little smile, "is Miss Althea Tower."

Amanda's eyes went wide. She stood up straight. She said, in a voice that cracked in the middle, "The Prophet?"

"That's right. You know she's very unwell, and the girl we hired to take care of her is leaving. You could stay with her, couldn't you? You were so good with the professor."

In just five seconds, Amanda had become a whole new person. Her face shone with eagerness. She straightened her shoulders, hooked a stray lock of hair behind her ear. "I could do it," she said. "I'd really *like* to!"

"Wonderful," said Mrs. Beeson. "If you can get ready, I'll take you over there right now and see if we can make an arrangement."

Nickie could see that Mrs. Brenda Beeson was the kind of person who moved fast and made firm decisions. She seemed nice, too. So after Amanda went upstairs, Nickie decided to ask some questions. But before she could say anything, there was a sudden pealing of tiny bells. Mrs. Beeson put her phone to her ear.

"Hello? Yes, Doralee, what is it?" She listened. "No, dear, I'm afraid not." A pause. "I know you're anxious, but, honey, Althea cannot see people's futures on demand. No. She is a prophet, not a fortune-teller." Another pause. "I'm sorry, Doralee dear, but it's out of the question. Please don't ask me again." She put down the phone and sighed. "I get these requests all the time," she said. "People are so nervous."

Nickie plunged ahead with her question. "Mrs. Beeson," she said, "do you think something terrible is going to happen? Like in the Prophet's vision?"

"Well, I don't want to scare you, honey," said Mrs. Beeson, "but I'm afraid it might. There's a lot of people in the world right now who want to hurt us. The forces of evil are strong. But our country is standing up against them, and here in Yonwood we are, too." She picked up the peanut butter jar and the loaf of bread and put them back in the cupboard. She brushed some crumbs off the table. "Our Prophet," she said, "is helping us."

"I know," said Nickie. "Amanda told me."

"Did she tell you about the hotline?" Mrs. Beeson asked. "It's a recorded phone message. Every day, people can call seven-seven-seven to hear her latest words and learn what to do about them. If there's something urgent, I can buzz their phones so they all get the message immediately. I arranged it all with my DATT phone." She showed Nickie the little phone, which had more tiny screens and buttons and sliding bits than any phone Nickie had seen. "I love high-tech gadgets, don't you? DATT stands for Do A Thousand Things. It doesn't really do quite a thousand, but just about." She pressed a button. "Wait a sec, that's the temperature." She pressed another button. "There we go. Nearly eleven. Where is that girl? I need to get going."

But Nickie wasn't through asking questions. She spoke quickly. "You know what, Mrs. Beeson?" she said. "I really want to do something to help the world."

"Then you've come to the right place," said Mrs. Beeson, putting her phone back in her pocket. She smiled. "Everyone here is trying to help the world. We're all quite passionate about it. We've had so many town meetings and church discussions and special votes—well, dangerous times bring people together. There are still a few who cling to their selfish ways, though, and that's very troubling. Even one can ruin everything, just the way one moldy strawberry in a basket can mess up all the rest."

Amanda's steps sounded on the stairs, and Mrs. Beeson stood up. But Nickie had to ask one more question. "What should I do?"

Mrs. Beeson was pulling on her jacket. She stuck her red cap on her head and pulled her ponytail out through the gap in the back. "Do?" she said. "Well, let's see. You might let me know if you happen to notice any trouble spots."

"You mean," Nickie said, "a trouble spot might be like—like what?"

Amanda came into the kitchen. "Here I am," she said. She had on nice clothes, and her hair was carefully combed.

"You look lovely, honey," said Mrs. Beeson. "I'll go and get my car. Meet me in front of the house."

"But Mrs. Beeson," said Nickie urgently. "What would a trouble spot be?"

Mrs. Beeson paused in the doorway. Her eyes grew serious. "You look for sinners, Nickie," she said. "It's one of the things the Prophet says most often: 'No sinners,' she says. 'No sinners.'"

"Sinners?" said Nickie. "You mean like lawbreakers?"

"Yes, but not *only* them," said Mrs. Beeson. "Sometimes they're not actually breaking a law, and still you have a sense of wrongness about them. You can just *feel* it." Mrs. Beeson paused for a moment to zip up her jacket. "Do you know of the man named Hoyt McCoy? Who lives down on Raven Road?"

"No," said Nickie. "I don't know anyone."

"No, of course you wouldn't. But he's an example. There's something about him—a whiff of wrongness. It's very strong." She started down the hall but stopped and looked back. "Do you love God?"

Nickie was surprised. "Sure," she said. "I guess so." The truth was, she had never thought about it. Her parents hadn't taken her to church, so she didn't know much about God.

"Excellent," said Mrs. Beeson. "We have to love God more than anything else. If you do, then you'll do fine. You can help us build a shield of goodness."

With another beaming smile, she turned and headed out the door.

"Isn't this just amazing?" Amanda said when Mrs. Beeson had left. "I was so scared when she came to the door. I mean, she's a real nice person, but I thought sure she was going to send me to a home. I never thought something like *this* could happen. Me taking care of the Prophet! Whoo! Do I look all right?"

"You look fine," said Nickie. "But what about Otis?"

"Oh, Lord, Otis," Amanda said. "Can you take care of him? He might hurt my chances to get hired. Can you feed him? And take him outside a couple times a day? Just for a little while? Please, please, *please*?"

And of course Nickie said she would.

As soon as Amanda had gone off with Mrs. Beeson, Nickie found a pencil and a scrap of paper and wrote down these words: *Sinners. Wrongness. Forces of evil. Shield of goodness.* Those were the things to remember. It was so perfect—she could accomplish her Goal #3 by helping to battle the forces of evil and build the shield of goodness. Just the very words made her feel like a warrior. Maybe she should give something up, the way everyone else was. If she did, would she have more love to give to God? She thought probably her love for God was a little weak, since she didn't know much about him and hadn't really thought about whether she loved him or not. It was hard to love someone invisible that you'd never met. Giving up something might strengthen her devotion. What could she give up? She'd think about it.

Then she ran up to the nursery to see Otis. She knelt down and held him up by his front paws so that they could look at each other eye to eye. "Otis," she said, "Amanda had to go away. I'm taking care of you now. Okay?" Otis gazed back at her. His eyes were like shiny deep-brown marbles. He cocked his head, as if trying to make sense of her words.

It was going to be a little tricky, taking care of Otis. She'd have to keep Crystal from coming up to the third floor. And she'd have to feed Otis and take him outside without letting Crystal see him. She hated leaving him all alone in the nursery room with nothing to do but chew things up. Did dogs get depressed from being alone too much? She didn't want Otis to be depressed. Luckily, it looked as if Crystal had so many errands to do and people to talk to that Nickie could probably be alone at Greenhaven for hours every day.

She pulled Otis onto her lap and hugged him. He wiggled out of her arms—his small blond body was amazingly strong—and then he sort of danced in front of her, his front paws stretched out straight and patting the air. "Woof!" he said, and Nickie instantly understood that *woof* meant *play*.

In the closet she found a little brown shoe that must have belonged to a child years ago. "Watch *this*, Otis!" she cried, and she threw the shoe across the room.

Otis hurled himself after it. He snatched up the shoe and raced back to her. He gave it a shake to make sure it was dead, and then he dropped it and waited, his round brown eyes on hers, shining with expectation.

They played Retrieve the Shoe for a long time, until Otis got distracted by a spider on the floor. Nickie went downstairs for another cup of hot chocolate and got back to find Otis in a squatting position, his back humped and his tail up and a faraway look in his eyes. Just in time, she seized an old magazine, put it under his rear end, and caught what came out before it could stain the rug.

Take him outside twice a day, Amanda had said. She'd forgotten. She found a leash hanging in the closet, hooked it to Otis's collar, and led him downstairs and out the kitchen door.

While he trotted among the bushes, she looked around. There was a clothesline back here and a concrete terrace bordered by a low stone wall. In the back of the house was a door that probably led to the basement. She tried it, but it was locked.

Once Otis was emptied out, they went back upstairs to the nursery. Nickie wondered if Amanda was having her interview with the Prophet at this very moment. She was so curious about the Prophet. She longed to meet her.

It was almost noon, but Crystal wasn't back yet, so Nickie went into the next room, one of the rooms crammed with trunks and boxes. Moving aside a stack of old magazines, she opened the biggest, oldest-looking trunk and saw a great jumble of stuff—mostly papers—inside. She scooped up an armful and took it back to the nursery room to look through.

No one had bothered to put any of these things in order, or even to store them neatly so they didn't get bent and crumpled. There were a lot of old Christmas cards, some faded snapshots of babies, and bunches of ancient bills and report cards and school papers. Toward the bottom of the pile, she found an envelope so old that its edges had come apart. Inside was a photograph on cardboard backing. She had just time to glance at it, and to notice that something about it was odd but she wasn't sure what, when she saw Crystal's car pull up outside. Nickie put the photograph back in its envelope. She scooped her piles off the window seat and put them in the toy cabinet, where Otis couldn't get at them. "Now, you sleep," she said to Otis. She left the room, closed the door behind her, and crammed some rags under it. Then she raced downstairs.

Crystal was just coming in the front door. She took her coat off and hung it on the coatrack in the hall. "Well, I met the real estate agent," she said. "Len Caldwell, his name is. Quite nice and helpful. He's very tall and has a funny little mustache." She smiled at Nickie. "And what's been happening here?"

Nickie opened her mouth and then quickly closed it. "Oh, I've just been wandering around," she said. "I love how big and spacious this house is, don't you?"

"It's big, all right," said Crystal. "There *is* something nice about having space to spread out. Of course, it's just more space that has to be cleaned."

Nickie was about to mention the beautiful curving staircase and the view of mountains from the back windows—but just then the phone rang.

Crystal picked it up. "Hello?" she said. "Rachel! How are you?"

It was Nickie's mother.

"Uh-huh," said Crystal. "Uh-huh, uh-huh. I know, it's really hard."

"I want to talk to her!" Nickie whispered loudly.

"You did?" said Crystal. "What did it say?"

"What did *what* say?" Nickie said.

"Huh," said Crystal. "Odd. Here, tell Nickie; she wants to know."

"Mom!" said Nickie into the phone. "Are you okay?"

"I'm okay," said her mother's weary voice. "I got a postcard from your father."

"You did? What did he say?"

"Not much. I hope he's all right. I just wish I knew where he was."

"Read it to me," Nickie said. "But wait a sec—I need to find a pencil. I want to write it down."

So her mother read her the postcard, and Nickie wrote down what she said. Then they talked for a while about her mother's job, about bomb alerts in the city, and about how cold it was. Nickie said how much she loved Greenhaven, and what a terrible mistake it would be to sell it. When they said goodbye, Nickie would have felt sad if she hadn't had the words of the postcard to study:

Dear Rachel and Nickie,

    All is fine here. Work is going well. Wish I could tell you where I am, but it's strictly forbidden.

        My love to you both, Dad

P.S. Three sparrows came to the bird feeder today!

Her mother was right. It didn't say much. Though it did tell her something new about her father—she hadn't known he was interested in birds at all.

CHAPTER 7

The Short Way Home

Grover couldn't concentrate at school that day. The classrooms were alive with whispers about the terrorist in the woods, and the bloody letter, and what Brenda Beeson said it meant. Even his teacher seemed nervous, Grover thought. She kept glancing out the window, and twice she came up with the wrong answers to the problems she was explaining.

After school, still more kids surrounded Grover and asked him to describe what he'd seen. He wished he could tell them that the Prophet herself had come to examine the bloody cloth. She was the one they were curious about. But no one had seen her since she'd had her vision—besides the doctor, no one but Mrs. Beeson and her small, devoted group. Grover remembered seeing Althea Tower in the bookshop sometimes before her vision, but she hadn't been interesting then—just a sort of fluffy-haired woman with rimless glasses and dust on her fingertips from handling used books. She'd always smiled at him when he went in there, but she never said much. She was pale, as he recalled, and wispy, and had a quiet voice.

But now he'd like to get a glimpse of her, to see if her eyes looked scorched and her hair frizzled like electric wires, to see if her face looked blasted, or frozen into astonishment, or whatever look there might be on the face of a person who had been shown a vision by God. If it really was God—Grover didn't know, and mostly he didn't care, as long as the results didn't affect him.

He ended up spending so much time talking to the kids in the schoolyard that he was in danger of getting home late. He was supposed to be home by three-thirty to help his grandmother with the kids; if he got home after his mother did, she'd tell his father, and his father was sure to yell at him. So he decided to do something he rarely did, because it was a bit of a risk: take the short way home.

The short way home was through Hoyt McCoy's backyard. Actually, *backyard* was too small a word for it; Hoyt McCoy's house lay within a large and brambly acreage. He had two or three times more land than most of his neighbors. At the rear part of it, a few slats of the fence had fallen sideways, making a hole big enough for a skinny boy to get through. Grover, holding his schoolbooks close to his chest, was just skinny enough.

Crossing Hoyt's yard cut a good five minutes off the time it took to get home. Grover knew this because he'd done it a few times before. The only risky part was at the back corner of the property, where the house stood. Here he would be within view of some windows, if anyone happened to be standing by them. But so much overgrown shrubbery grew up the back of the house, and the windows were so coated with dust and grime, that he didn't think the chance of being seen was very great.

This time, though, he was wrong. As he came up behind the house, staying as close to the fence as he could and trying not to crunch too much on the fallen leaves, an upstairs window flew open. The deep voice of Hoyt McCoy rang out.

"Halt, trespasser! I have you in my sights! Vacate these premises instantly!"

Grover stopped so fast that he dropped his books. He froze, hoping the bushes would hide him. He waited, watching the open window. Did Hoyt mean he had a rifle trained on him? Would he actually shoot it? Grover didn't know. So he stayed where he was until finally the window closed. Then he waited a little longer, and at last he bent to pick his books up and moved on, staying in the shadows, setting each foot down with great care, until he came to the gravel drive that led out to the street. Then he ran.

Hoyt McCoy was one of Yonwood's oddities. He'd moved there about ten years ago from a university town somewhere. For a year or so after he'd bought the house, workers from out of town had come every day, and sounds of drilling and sawing and hammering had issued from inside. People thought maybe Hoyt's family was coming to live with him—but no. Hoyt lived alone. Sometimes he went away for weeks at a time, leaving the gate across his driveway padlocked. When he was at home, he seemed almost never to have visitors, although a few times Grover had seen a dark green sedan turning in at his driveway, in which there were always two men in suits. They were probably tax collectors, Grover thought. It wasn't likely Hoyt McCoy would have friends. He was tall and gaunt, with caved-in cheeks and dark hollows around his eyes. He walked with his shoulders stooped and his head craned forward, as if he were looking for something to pounce on—and in his way, he did pounce on things. Everything met with his disapproval. On days when Hoyt showed up at the market or the post office or the drugstore, Grover had seen him tut-tutting at loud children, shaking his fist at cars that came too close to him, and scolding clerks for being rude. He also scoffed at everything Mrs. Beeson said about the

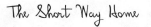

Prophet's vision. "Orders from heaven," he would say, pursing his lips. "Nonsense. *She* doesn't know. I'm the expert on heaven, not her. If you want to know about celestial matters, ask me." But no one ever did ask him, as far as Grover could see. Hardly anyone ever spoke to him at all, if they could help it.

When Grover got home, only a little bit late, he found his grandmother in the living room in her usual spot, the armchair by the heater, with a baby on her lap. All around her, little kids of various ages crawled and toddled, babbled and cried and screeched. The TV was on. A newsman was saying that the president had set a deadline of one week, exactly seven days, for the Phalanx Nations to deactivate their missiles. Otherwise, the United States would have no choice but to—

His grandmother aimed the remote and flicked off the TV. "Heard there's more trouble in town," she said.

Grover dumped his books on a side table. "I was the first one there, Granny Carrie," he said. "I was the one who told Andy."

"Good for you," said his grandmother. "On top of things as usual."

One of Grover's little brothers whacked his sister with a stuffed animal. The little girl wailed. The baby on his grandmother's lap started to cry.

This was how it always was at Grover's house. He

had six brothers and sisters, all younger, who created a constant uproar. His father worked as a handyman, and his mother worked at the dress shop, so his grandmother was the one who minded the children. Grover had to mind them, too, when he came home from school. All of this meant he was always short of time—time for homework, and time for other things that were more important to him than homework.

"Look here, Grover," Granny Carrie said. "I found some good ones for you." She leaned over and picked up a stack of magazines from the floor. "There's one that gets you ten thousand dollars. Another one gets you a car, but you could trade that for cash."

"Great," said Grover. He took the top magazine and opened it to the page his grandmother had dog-eared. "The Fabulous Dorfberry Sweepstakes!" it said in big red letters. "Hundreds of Prizes! Grand Prize $10,000!" He read the fine print. All you had to do was collect five box tops from Dorfberry's Cornmeal Products and fill out an entry blank. Easy. His family ate a ton of corn muffins and cornbread. He could collect five box tops in less than a week.

"For this one here," said Granny Carrie, opening another magazine, "you have to write a paragraph." She showed it to him. "Why buy Armstrong Pickles?" said the ad. "You tell us! One hundred words or less." The grand prize was five hundred dollars, which would be more than enough.

"This is good," said Grover, moving the magazine away from the reaching fingers of his littlest brother. "Thanks. I'll probably win a whole lot of these and have money left over. I'll buy you a Cadillac."

"You better not," said Granny Carrie. "You can buy me some new slippers. These ones are getting worn out." She stuck out her feet, on which she was wearing yellow slippers with duck heads on them. They were a little ragged around the edges.

"Okay," said Grover. He'd be happy to buy his grandmother anything she wanted.

At five-thirty his mother came home, looking tired and carrying a bag of groceries. "Somebody's lurking around in the woods," she said, setting the bag down and taking off her coat.

"I know it," said Grover.

"Don't you go up there," she said. "You stay around here for a change." She started taking boxes and cans from the bag and putting them away.

A little later, Grover's father came home. He came in the back door, leaving his toolbox on the porch. "Hear about the break-in?" he said.

"Yes," said everyone.

"Gurney and his men ought to get up there in the woods and flush that guy out," said Grover's father. "Take their rifles with them."

"Don't talk about rifles," said Grover's mother. "It scares me."

His father just shrugged. "Serious times call for serious solutions," he said.

"A shield of goodness is a better protection," his mother said.

"Fine," said his father. "You work on being good; I'll keep the gun loaded."

"It could be just some poor wandering tramp up there," said his grandmother.

"Trouble is," said his father, "we don't *know*. He could be a tramp; he could be a guy scoping out bomb sites. Do you want to take the risk?"

Grover noticed a smear of grease on the side of his father's neck. Probably he'd been doing a plumbing job today. He could do just about anything—plumbing, carpentry, electrical work. He always had a lot of jobs, and he always came home tired and slightly grumpy in the evening.

"I'm going down to the shed," said Grover. There was still at least half an hour before dinner, and he wanted to use it.

"Now, listen here," said his father. "You waste a lot of time fooling around in that shed. What about your homework? Don't tell me you don't have any."

"I do, but I can do it later," Grover said.

"What comes first, getting ready for your future or fiddling with your little hobbies?" Grover's father put one foot up on a chair and untied his shoe. "If you're going to do something useful with your life, you've got to get started."

"I *am* going to do something useful," Grover said.

"Not the way you're going, you're not," said his father, untying the other shoe and letting it thump to the floor. He started in on the rant Grover had heard a thousand times. "You have to think *practical*. The world is headed for disaster; I think we can say that for sure. But afterward, assuming the human race survives, there's going to be a big need for builders, architects, engineers. Study a little harder, and you could be one of them."

But Grover had other ideas. He picked up his books and went back to his room. He flopped onto his bed. Instead of going down to the shed, he'd put the finishing touches on his application tonight, the one that was going to change his life. It was in the slim blue notebook he carried with him everywhere.

But where was the notebook? He had his English book, his math book, his history book—but not his blue notebook. Had he left it at school? He wouldn't have done that. Could he have—? A terrible thought struck him.

His blue notebook—he suddenly knew—was lying in the weeds behind the horrible house of Hoyt McCoy.

CHAPTER 8

A Crack in the Sky

He was going to have to go tonight, while it was dark. Otherwise, Hoyt would see him and try to shoot him again. This gave Grover a queasy feeling in his stomach, which made it hard to eat his dinner. When dinner was over and the little kids were in bed, his parents settled on the couch and flicked on the TV. A government spokesman was talking about the deadline the president had set for the Phalanx Nations to agree to the United States' demands, and that if the demands weren't met, the consequences would be serious, but no one should be alarmed, because emergency measures were planned, and—

"I'm going outside for a while," Grover said.

"All right," his mother said without looking at him. "Be back in by nine-thirty."

Grover went out the back door as if he were going across the yard to his shed, but instead he circled around the side of the house and headed down the street. Lucky it wasn't raining, he thought. Rain would turn his blue notebook into a soggy rag. And lucky the moon was just a sliver in the sky, shedding hardly any light. That would help him hide from Hoyt's sharp eyes.

Grover hurried downhill. He wanted to get this over with. If he hadn't already filled in so much of the application form, he could just leave it there and send for another one. But he'd put in hours trying to get it just right. And besides, the deadline was only a week away. He wouldn't have time to send for another one, get it done, and turn it in on time. He had to find the one he'd lost.

He passed the last house on his street and turned left onto Raven Road. It was darker here, because there were fewer houses shining the light from their windows out into the night. In less than five minutes, he came to the drive that led back into Hoyt's land and started walking up it. His shoes crunched on the gravel, a sound that seemed much too loud. He tried to walk on the edge of the drive, where the gravel merged into dirt, but his feet kept getting tangled in the brambles that grew there.

He crept along to the left, moving toward the back of the house, staying as close to the fence as he could. The house loomed tall and dark—only one window on the top story was lit. With thorns and stickers catching at his sleeves, Grover made his way through the thickets of brush to the place where, that afternoon, he'd frozen at the sound of Hoyt's voice. He was sure this was where he'd dropped his books; his notebook should still be right there on the ground, as long as Hoyt hadn't found it and thrown it in the trash, or some animal hadn't taken it away to shred for its nest. There was a straight line of sight from here to the top window of the house, the one that now glowed yellow around the edges of the drawn shade.

He dropped to his knees. Where was the darned thing? The shadows of the trees and bushes were so thick here that he could hardly see at all. He'd have to find it by feel. He ran his hands over the ground. Pebbles, clumps of cold dirt, scratchy weeds, dry fallen leaves. But no notebook. He held back a groan of frustration. He *had* to find it, because if he didn't find it, he wouldn't be able to go, even if he *did* get the money, and he *had* to go, because his whole future depended on it, and he was *furious* with himself for dropping it, and—

At that moment, his fingers touched something smooth. He reached farther and felt the spiral wires. His notebook. He grabbed it and stood up. Carefully, he riffled the pages, feeling for the loose one. Yes, it was there, tucked into the middle, just where he'd put it. All right. Now to get out of there.

He turned back toward the driveway and felt his

way forward between the tree trunks and the brush. He crept behind Hoyt's black car, parked near the corner of the house. At the spot where he'd have to go out into the open, he paused and checked the house again. It was still all dark except for the rectangle of light around the top-floor window. But as he watched, the light went out. Startled, Grover stepped back into the shadows and stood still for a moment. It might just be that Hoyt had turned off his light to sleep. Or it might be that he'd heard something and was about to peer out his window. Grover waited and watched—and an odd thing happened.

At first he thought he was imagining it, it was so faint. A light seemed to be growing behind the curtained and shuttered windows on the ground floor. It was a bluish light, like moonlight. It gleamed very faintly around the edges of the windows, in the gaps between the shades and the frames, until a narrow, pale-bluish rectangle appeared around all the ground-floor windows. What was it? Did Hoyt have twenty televisions that went on all at once? Was he doing some weird sort of experiment? Whatever it was, it gave Grover an eerie feeling.

He stood still for a moment, staring. Then, as if his ears had suddenly been stuffed with cotton, the whole world seemed to go silent, and in the sky over Hoyt McCoy's house, a brilliant line, thin as a wire, shot across the darkness. It was there for less than a second.

It vanished, and the sounds came back—rustling leaves, a distant calling bird. But Grover had seen it— it wasn't his imagination. It had looked like a long, narrow crack, as if the two great round halves of the night sky had slid apart just for a second, just enough to let through a light that was on the other side. It was the strangest thing he had ever seen.

But nothing else happened. The blue light continued to shine behind the windows; the house was silent; the sky stayed black. After another few minutes, Grover clutched his notebook tightly and moved toward the driveway, quiet as a cat and slow, until he got far enough from the house. Then he dashed along the driveway's edge down to Raven Road, where he set out for home.

CHAPTER 9

At the Prophet's House

Saturday morning, Crystal bustled everywhere, check-
ing on things, adding items to her list. Plumbers
arrived and began clanking away in the kitchen and in
the bathrooms. Painters arrived and started sanding
down windowsills and spreading out tarps in the
parlor. Crystal marched from room to room, giving
directions.

Now and then people stopped by to tell her how
sorry they were about Professor Green. Some of them
stood chatting for a long time. Nickie could see that
they were curious about Crystal and maybe a little suspicious. They asked her all kinds of questions—"Are
you married, dear?" "Will you be coming to live in
Yonwood?" "What church do you attend?" "Have you
met our Mrs. Beeson yet?"—until Crystal said it was
lovely talking with them, but she had so much to do
that she must say goodbye.

"I'm off to see some antique dealers," she said to Nickie when they were gone, "about selling some of this ghastly furniture. After that I have a meeting with the real estate agent. I'll see you sometime this afternoon."

As soon as Crystal had left, Nickie ran past the painters and up the stairs. She opened the hall door, then the nursery door, and there was Otis waiting for her, looking up with his round brown eyes and wagging his rear end, his short comma-shaped tail pointing at the ceiling. She took him downstairs and, when he was finished, brought him back inside. In the kitchen, she made herself a cup of hot chocolate. As she was doing that, the telephone rang.

She hardly ever answered the telephone here, since it was never for her. The answering machine answered if Crystal wasn't home. Usually the voice on the answering machine belonged to someone talking about house repairs. But this time the voice was Amanda's.

"Hello," it said. "Um . . . uh . . . Well, this is Amanda Stokes, and I . . . uh . . ."

Nickie snatched up the receiver. "Amanda!" she said. "It's me."

"Oh, good," said Amanda. "I didn't know what to say if it was your aunt getting the message."

"Did you get the job? With the Prophet?"

"I did!" said Amanda. "I am so lucky! But I'm calling up because I need my stuff. Can you bring it to me?"

"Sure," Nickie said. "Just tell me what to bring."

"It's all in my suitcase, under the bed. Except don't bring the books that are in there. Those are the ones I gave up. You can have them."

"Okay. I'll come right now. What's the Prophet's address?"

"It's 248 Grackle Street," Amanda said. She explained how to get there and said thanks, and Nickie hung up and did a little dance of excitement right there in the hall. She was going to see the Prophet's house! She was going to meet the Prophet herself!

She took Otis upstairs. She pulled out Amanda's suitcase from beneath the bed and opened it up, then rummaged through it to find the books (and also because she was curious). Underwear, socks, a striped flannel nightgown, some T-shirts, and a few pairs of pants. A floppy pink stuffed kitten, so old its fur was mostly worn away. A battered postcard with a picture of a beach. Nickie couldn't resist reading it. In big round handwriting, it said, "Dear Pumpkin, What a great place! Lots of beaches! See you soon, Your Mama." The date on the postcard was twelve years ago. Nickie wondered if this was all Amanda had of her mother.

She found the books underneath everything else. There were four of them, all paperbacks. She picked one up. On the cover was a woman with hair like a black waterfall, swooning in the arms of a man who was gazing at her hungrily. It was called *Heaven in His Arms*. Another one was called *A Heart in Flames*. Its cover showed a clasped-together couple standing on a windswept cliff with a blazing sunset in the sky behind them. All the books were like that. They looked interesting. She would read them herself. They might help her with Goal #2.

She put everything else back into the suitcase, went downstairs, edging past a carpenter repairing the front door, and set off for the Prophet's house.

It was a blustery morning. Big heaps of cloud rushed across the sky, and the wind was chilly. A few dead leaves skittered along the sidewalk. Nickie turned onto Main Street. Downtown, something seemed to be going on. Clusters of people stood here and there on the sidewalks, talking excitedly. As Nickie passed the drugstore, she saw that the TV inside was on, and people had gathered around it and were listening to the news. There were more people around the TV in the video store and also at the Cozy Corner Café. The president must be making some kind of announcement—she could see his solemn face and white hair on the screen—but she didn't want to stop and listen to him right now. She wanted to get on to the Prophet's house. Later she could find out what he'd said.

She walked four blocks up Grackle Street to number 248. It was a neat white house with a front porch, more or less like the other houses on the street, except that there were some bunches of limp flowers tied to the fence, along with a Christmas tree angel, a couple of holy-looking pictures, and a couple of handwritten signs. One said, "Althea, Our Prophet!" and the other one said, "We believe!" A bird feeder hung from the porch roof, but there were no seeds in it. The curtains in all the windows were closed.

Nickie rang the bell, and after a moment Amanda opened the door. "Oh, hi," she said, reaching for the suitcase. "Thanks for bringing this."

"You're welcome," Nickie said.

"Well," said Amanda. "See you later." She took a step back and started to close the door.

"But can't I come in?" Nickie said. "Can't I meet the Prophet?" She tried to look past Amanda into the room. Were there people in there? She thought she heard the sound of voices.

"Oh, gosh, no," said Amanda. Her eyebrows bunched into a worried line, and she backed up another step. "There's strict rules."

"Even if I just peeked in her door and said hello in a really soft voice?"

"Oh, yeah, even that. I can't let you," Amanda said. "I'd get in trouble."

"Well, who gets to visit her?"

"Just Mrs. Beeson and her committee. You know,

Reverend Loomis, and the mayor, and the police chief, and the others. One or two of them's here most of the time, sitting with her, in case she says something important," said Amanda. She glanced back over her shoulder. "A couple of 'em are here right now."

"Right now?"

"Yeah, having a meeting about stuff she's said."

"You mean she talks to them?"

"She sort of mumbles," Amanda said, "and then they hover over her and listen and whisper about what they think she said. And then they tiptoe out, and sometimes, like now, they stand around in the living room arguing about what she meant."

At that moment, a car pulled up at the curb.

"Uh-oh," Amanda said. "Mrs. Beeson is here. I got to get back to work."

Mrs. Beeson got out of her car and bustled up to the door. "Excuse me, dears," she said. "Urgent business." She pushed past them and disappeared into the house.

"I have to go," Amanda said. "But listen—how's Otis?"

"He's fine," Nickie said.

"I'm getting up my nerve to ask Mrs. Beeson if I can have him here," said Amanda.

Nickie's heart sank. She'd already forgotten that Otis wasn't hers.

"But I don't think she's going to let me," Amanda went on. "So I don't know. Do you think you—?"

"Oh, yes," said Nickie, relieved. "I'll take care of him. I don't mind at all. Don't worry about it." Her heart sprang up again. She said goodbye and headed down the path.

Clouds sailed across the sun, turning the day dark. She hurried to keep warm, down Grackle Street and past the park to Main Street. Maybe she could find out now what the president's announcement had been.

She made her way toward the Cozy Corner Café, thinking she could go in and ask someone there. But before she got there she heard a sort of buzz in the air, like a distant swarm of bees, and all around her people stopped in their tracks and pulled cell phones from their pockets and purses.

What was happening? It must be news from Mrs. Beeson, maybe about the "urgent business" that had taken her to the Prophet's house. She had to know. Who could she ask?

She spotted a red-haired boy wearing glasses with heavy frames. He was coming out of the café, carrying a doughnut, and had his phone pressed to his ear. He looked about her age, or a little older. She'd ask him.

She stepped up beside him and said, "Excuse me," into the ear that didn't have the phone against it.

He turned and looked at her.

"What's going on?" Nickie said. "Can you tell me?"

He frowned. "Wait," he said, holding up the hand with the doughnut. He was still listening intently. She waited. Finally, he folded up his phone.

"Who are you?" he said. "I don't know you."

She explained who she was. He stared at her suspiciously for a moment, but he must have decided she couldn't be a terrorist, because he said, "I'm Martin. Did you hear the president's announcement?"

"No," said Nickie. "What did he say?"

"Well, look," said Martin. "I've got it on my DATT." He flicked a tiny switch on his phone, and on a tiny screen the tiny face of the president appeared.

He looked grim. His face was grayish, as if he hadn't slept or eaten well for a while. "Six days remain," he said in a tiny version of his usual voice, "before time runs out for the Phalanx Nations. They have remained uncooperative. Therefore I am asking all directors of defense to activate their emergency plans, in case an attack is imminent." He went on about evacuations and shelters and troop movements, and he ended in the usual way: "Let us pray to God for the safety of our people and the success of our endeavors."

Nickie gulped. She looked up from the little screen. "So is that why—," she began. But she stopped, because something strange was happening. All up and down the street, the lights in the stores were going off.

One after another, the windows went dark. "What's going on?" she said.

"It's because of Mrs. Beeson's bulletin," said Martin. "She's just figured out a new instruction from the Prophet. See, for a long time the Prophet has been saying 'No lies,' or 'No lines,' or 'No lights,' but no one could tell which. Mrs. Beeson thought it was 'No lies,' because it's bad to tell lies. But now she realizes it must be 'No lights,' because that matches up with what the president just said."

"It does?"

"Obviously," said Martin, folding up his phone and putting it in his pocket. "The president is warning us about an attack. It might come any minute. If we turn our lights out, we won't be seen from the air."

Nickie looked up and down Main Street. It seemed almost like night, with all the windows dark and the sky clouded over. For the first time, she felt a real shiver of fear at the war that might come. It must have shown, because Martin said, "You shouldn't worry too much. There *is* destruction coming, but we're probably safe here."

"You mean because of the Prophet?"

"That's right. It's like having a phone line direct to God. As long as we follow directions, we should be okay. Even though there's a terrorist in the woods."

"There is?"

Martin nodded. "He broke into the restaurant just yesterday morning."

"That's awful," Nickie said. She had thought she'd escaped all that by coming to Yonwood. Clearly she'd been wrong.

Martin was peering at her as if trying to decide what kind of creature she was. "Do you love God?" he said.

Having been asked this question once before, Nickie was prepared. "Oh, yes!" she said. "I really do."

Martin smiled. His teeth were white and even, and Nickie noticed that his eyes, behind his glasses, were hazel, an interesting color that went well with his red hair. "That's good," he said. "Well, I have to get going. See you." He strode away, leaving Nickie standing there on the strangely darkened street, beneath the darkening sky. She felt excited and uneasy at the same time. She'd met a boy—that was progress on Goal #2. But the danger to the world had just gotten worse—which made Goal #3, doing something to help, more urgent than ever.

CHAPTER 10

The Photograph and the Journal

Nickie walked back to Greenhaven, thoughts zooming around in her mind like bees. So much had happened in just two days. She felt a little dizzy with it all. She would read for a while, she decided, to get calmed down.

Her plan for that afternoon was to go through the Look at Later pile. She went into the kitchen to make herself a cup of hot chocolate—and it occurred to her all at once that hot chocolate was the perfect thing to give up. It was something she really liked, so it would be *hard* to give up; and doing something hard would strengthen her goodness, just the way exercise strengthened muscles.

So she made a cup of mint tea instead and carried it up to the nursery, where she took her Look at Later pile from the toy cabinet and set it on the window seat. The light was dim there because of the blankets she and Amanda had hung over the windows, and because of the cloudy sky. She pushed one of the blankets aside a little and settled down with a big red pillow at her back. Otis jumped up next to her.

The first thing she wanted to check was that envelope she'd begun to look at yesterday. She picked it up and slid out the photograph. It was brownish and had a cardboard backing. It showed six people—two men and two women, seated, and two children sitting on the floor in front of them. They wore old-fashioned outfits and had sour looks on their faces, as if they were annoyed with the photographer for making them sit still so long.

The Messrs. Bunker and Their Wives, visitors to Greenhaven on June 4, 1858.

There was something odd about the two men, who sat next to each other in the center of the group. At first Nickie thought one of them was sitting in the other one's lap. She looked closer. The two men, who looked just alike, seemed to be stuck together. Yes! They were joined by what looked like a thick finger of flesh that went from the stomach of one to the stomach of the other. That was why they were sitting in that odd way. They were twins—connected twins, or something like that. There was another word for it that she couldn't remember.

Under the picture, someone had written, "The Mssrs. Bunker and Their Wives, visitors to Greenhaven on June 4, 1868."

Visitors to Greenhaven! They had been here, in this house. She gazed at the picture a long time. How would it be to live your life attached to someone else? You could never get away from each other, not to go for a walk, not in bed at night, not even in the bathroom! If one was sick, the other would have to lie there, too. If one wanted to go downtown and the other wanted to stay home and read the newspaper, they'd have to negotiate about it and try to agree. Each one would always hear everything the other one said. It was the strangest kind of life she could imagine.

She put the picture back in its envelope and took up the small brown notebook that Amanda had brought to her, the one her great-grandfather had written in.

She read the first entry again, where he said he'd been having odd experiences, and then she read on.

12/10 It's the second-floor bedroom, I think, the one at the west end of the hall. Why there? Some memory being triggered? Can't figure it out.

12/13 Darn hip giving me trouble. Stayed in bed most of the day.

12/19 Althea T. still not speaking much after nearly six months. Brenda B. very worried about her.

He was writing about the Prophet! But then the next entry was about something quite different:

12/27 Could past, present, and future all exist at the same time? And certain people slip around between them? See theories set forth in recent sci. journals. Ask M.

Hmmm. What was that about?

A movement on the sidewalk below caught her attention. She looked out the window. There was Mrs. Beeson, wearing a rain jacket with the hood up over her baseball cap, walking a long-bodied, short-legged dog on a leash. That must be Sausage, Nickie thought. She watched as Mrs. Beeson passed, walked on, and turned in at a house across the street. It was a brick house, old but well cared for, with a straight path that led to a white front door with a tall, narrow window on each side. Two bushes flanked the door, both of them trimmed into neat round shapes like green beach balls. It was a perfect-looking house, Nickie thought, just right for Mrs. Beeson, who was aiming to get rid of all the wrongness in Yonwood. If only the whole *world* could be that way!

She watched until Mrs. Beeson and Sausage had disappeared into the house. Then she lay back on the big red pillow to think for a while, and the next thing she knew, it was twilight outside and Crystal's voice was calling from downstairs.

She leapt up and rushed out of the room, not forgetting to cram the rags under the door, and she sped downstairs before Crystal could come up looking for her.

"What a day!" Crystal said. She hung her coat on the coatrack that stood in the hall. "I've been all over the place. What have you been doing? Just reading?"

"Mostly," said Nickie.

"Found anything interesting?"

"Lots," Nickie said. "This house is just full of inter-esting stuff. I don't see how you can stand to sell it!"

Crystal just shrugged. "Interesting stuff like what?" she said.

"I found a really strange old photograph, for one thing. Wait a second and I'll show you."

She dashed upstairs again. Otis trotted over to her when she went in. Feeling sorry that he'd be alone from now till morning, she knelt down and patted him for a while. She rumpled his ears and, when he rolled over, scratched his stomach. Then she took the picture of the twins from its envelope and hurried back down-stairs, where she found Crystal talking on the phone.

"Try not to worry," Crystal said. "I'm sure he's fine. Okay. Okay. Bye." She hung up. "That was your mother," she said.

Nickie cried, "But I wanted to talk to her!"

"She was exhausted," said Crystal, "too tired to talk. She just wanted to let us know that she's had another postcard from your father. I wrote it down for you." She handed Nickie a scrap of paper.

Nickie read:

Dear Rachel and Nickie,

We are working hard here on a big project.

I am well, and I hope both of you are, too. I miss you.

love, Dad

P.S. Sure would like to have one of Rachel's peanut

butter cookies right now!

Again, not much news. But also again, a puzzling P.S. She couldn't remember her mother *ever* making peanut butter cookies. What was going on in her father's mind?

Crystal had gone into the kitchen, and Nickie followed her. "Here's the picture," she said, putting it on the table.

"Oh, yes!" Crystal said. "I remember hearing about this! These men are Chang and Eng, who came from Siam—that's what we now call Thailand. They were the original 'Siamese twins.' They came to the United States and traveled around being exhibited for years, and then they retired to North Carolina, not far from here. Grandfather told me they'd visited this house once—it was at the time of his great-grandfather, sometime after the Civil War. They must have given this photo to the family as a sort of thank-you gift." She turned the photograph over. "Look at this!" she exclaimed. "They've written on the back."

Nickie peered at the old-fashioned handwriting. It

said, "With gratitude for your hospitality," and it was signed with two names.

"If this is authentic," said Crystal, "it could be worth something."

"How much?" said Nickie.

"I have no idea. Not a great deal, probably, but something."

Nickie took the photo and turned it over again. "I guess those two boys are their children," she said.

"Yes," said Crystal. "In fact, I think they had something like ten children apiece."

"Wouldn't it be hard to be married to Siamese twins?" said Nickie, looking at the grumpy faces of the two big women.

"I surely think so," said Crystal. "In fact, as I recall, the two women were sisters, but they didn't get along. After a while, the twins got themselves two houses, one for each wife, and the husbands alternated between them." She shook her head. "Amazing, isn't it, that they managed to work things out at all? I tried twice, under much easier circumstances, and failed both times." She opened up a cupboard and took down a can of soup. "Can you bear to have soup again for dinner?" she said. "I'm too tired to do anything else."

"That's okay," said Nickie. She wondered if she should tell Crystal about the Prophet, and Mrs. Beeson, and how Yonwood was battling the forces of evil by building a shield of goodness. But she hesitated. Crystal might decide that Nickie shouldn't be getting involved in that battle. She might decide that Nickie needed more supervision. Nickie didn't want that at all. So all she said was, "Crystal, do you think there's going to be a war?"

"I don't know," Crystal said. "Fortunately, I'm too busy to think much about it." She cast a quick look at Nickie. "Don't *you* think about it, either," she said. "There's not much we can do."

"Just live good lives, right?" Nickie said. "Not add to the badness. That's what you said before."

"Uh-huh," said Crystal. She opened the can and scooped the soup into a pot.

"So if *everyone* lives good lives, then maybe bad things won't happen," Nickie said. "At least not to us." But she could tell Crystal wasn't really listening. She was holding the soup can under the faucet to fill it, but only a feeble trickle of water was coming out.

"Something is wrong with the water pressure," she said. "We must have a leaky pipe somewhere. And the plumbers were just here! They've made it worse instead of better. And of course tomorrow is Sunday, so a plumber will be hard to find." She sighed. "There's *so* much to do. I suppose I should face the third floor. I haven't even been up there."

Nickie's heart jumped into her throat. "It's just

rooms full of boxes," she said. "You don't need to see it."

"No, I really should." Crystal stirred the soup with one hand and ran the other hand wearily through her hair. "I need to see what I have to deal with. Not tonight, though. I'll do it first thing tomorrow morning." Crystal reached for two bowls. "It's getting dark," she said. "Would you switch the light on?"

That was when Nickie remembered. "We have to close all the curtains and blinds," she said.

"We do? Why?"

"So we can't be seen from the air," said Nickie. "In case there's an attack." She pulled down the kitchen blinds.

"Oh, I don't think that's necessary," Crystal said. "But if it makes you feel better, go ahead."

Nickie went from room to room, closing curtains and blinds all over the house.

CHAPTER 11

Trouble Spots

The next morning after breakfast, as soon as Crystal had washed her dishes and disappeared into the bathroom, Nickie raced upstairs. She hooked Otis to his leash and flew down the stairs again. She tiptoed past Crystal's room, where she heard the roar of the hair dryer, and zipped out the back door.

At the far end of the garden, she looped Otis's leash around the trunk of a tree. "Now, Otis," she said, "try to be quiet. I'll come back for you as soon as I can."

Inside again, past Crystal's room (this time she heard the *pssst-pssst* of the hair spray), up the stairs to the nursery. She hid the dog dishes and the dog food in a box of old toys in the closet, tore down the blanket that they'd hung over the door—and then came Crystal's steps on the stairs, and her voice calling, "Are you up there?"

Nickie showed her the two storage rooms first. "Oh, horrors," said Crystal, looking at the cobwebby trunks and boxes and suitcases. "It's *true* that they never threw anything away. Just looking at it gives me a headache." She went toward the nursery. "What's in here?"

"I've been sort of staying in here," Nickie said.

Crystal strode in. She gazed at the rugs, the blankets hung on the walls, the rocking chair and lamps.

"I did it," Nickie said. "I wanted to make it cozy."

Crystal smiled at her. "Well, it is cozy," she said. "It's actually quite a nice room. It smells a little funny, though." She wrinkled her nose. "Probably there are rats up under the roof. Let's let some air in." She went to the window and thrust it open. The sound of barking and whining floated up from below, but Crystal paid no attention. "When we get ready to put the house on the market," she said, "we can sell this as a perfect space for a home gym. Or maybe a media center. Screen over there"—she raised her hands, measuring a wall-sized screen—"theater seats here. Could be quite lovely. What do you think?"

But she didn't pause to hear what Nickie thought (which was that she didn't like any of those ideas). She went right on to say that she would decide what to do about all this later, but today, since it was Sunday and she couldn't do much shopping, she was going to take a drive with Len. "I don't suppose you want to come," she said.

"Who's Len?" said Nickie.

"The real estate agent."

"Oh," said Nickie. "No, I don't want to come."

Once Crystal had left, Nickie rescued Otis from the back garden and played with him a long time to make up for his exile. The shoe they'd been using for a toy had turned into a shapeless wad by now, so Nickie found an ancient yellow tennis ball in the closet. Otis adored it. He had to stretch his jaws wide apart to hold it, which made him look as if he were trying to swallow a grapefruit.

When Otis lost interest in chasing the ball and settled down to gnaw on it, Nickie decided that today would be her day to explore Yonwood. It was going to be her home, after all, if she accomplished her Goal #1. And while she was at it, she would keep her eyes open for sinners and trouble spots and anything that had a feeling of wrongness. If she was going to accomplish Goal #3, she needed to understand all this. She would keep her eyes open for Martin, too. She might happen to run into him somewhere, and they might happen to talk to each other. She needed to find out if he was someone she could fall in love with (Goal #2). So far, she couldn't tell. He was nice-looking. He was friendly, sort of. That was enough for a start.

She walked to the upper end of Main Street, where the school was, empty today because it was Sunday. Though it was still cold and windy, the sun was out. Some boys were shooting baskets in the schoolyard. She looked to see if Martin was one of them, but he was not.

A few blocks farther on and she was in downtown Yonwood. A few stores were open, but their lights were still off. They looked uninviting, like dim caves. Small clusters of people gathered in places where a TV was on, showing the news. Nickie heard snippets as she passed: "Five days remaining until the deadline . . . ," said the president's voice from the Cozy Corner Café. "Ambassador has been assassinated," he said from the newsstand. "Group calling itself the Warriors of God has claimed . . . ," he said from the drugstore. The familiar nervous feeling started up in Nickie's stomach as she heard these words, and she could tell that other people were nervous, too. A woman behind her was talking about how the tension was just killing her, and another woman answered that it was killing her, too, but that they had to have faith that they'd be all right, and the first person said, Yes, she did believe that, but she just wished everyone did. . . . Nickie hurried on, not wanting to hear any more.

Half a block down, she suddenly heard the strange

hum she'd heard before: *MMMM-mmmm-MMMM-mmmm.* Where was it coming from? A machine inside a building? Some kind of car or engine on the street? She looked around but saw nothing. The hum grew slightly louder. Was it behind the grocery store? She peered up a narrow alley and thought she saw someone darting across the other end—but she wasn't sure. The hum faded.

Nickie turned around. Behind her were two of the people who'd been watching the president at the drugstore a minute ago: a short bald man and a gray-haired woman. "Did you hear that funny sound?" she said. "Do you know what it was?"

Neither one answered. They kept on walking. The man cast a suspicious glance at her, and the woman pressed her lips together and shook her head.

"I just wondered—," Nickie said.

The woman stopped and glared at her. "You should *know,*" she said. "Why don't you know? Whose child *are* you?" But she didn't wait for an answer. She reached for the man's arm, and they hastened away.

Nickie felt as if she'd been slapped. She wasn't supposed to ask about the hum; that was clear. But why not? How was she supposed to find out if she didn't ask?

She went on. Toward the end of Main Street she came to the grocery store, and beyond that was the church she'd seen when she and Crystal had first arrived. "The Church of the Fiery Vision," the sign said, but she could also make out the old name that had been crossed out: "Yonwood Community Church." Today the sign also said, "Today's Sermon: Pulling Together in Dark Times." A lot of people were gathered here, milling about and greeting one another in low voices. Many of them were wearing the round blue button she'd first seen on Mrs. Beeson. The doors of the church stood open, and beside them was a thin-faced man dressed in a sort of robe, dark blue with a white border. Was that the Reverend Loomis? Nickie wondered. She saw Mrs. Beeson standing near him, though she almost didn't recognize her at first, because Mrs. Beeson was wearing a woolly gray hat like an upside-down bowl, and her hair was brushed and fluffy instead of in a ponytail. She spoke to all the people as they went inside. Nickie waved to her, and Mrs. Beeson flashed her a smile.

Nickie turned around and walked back the way she'd come, but on the other side of the street this time. She noticed a few things that might be examples of wrongness. By the park, she saw an old man spitting on the sidewalk. Surely that was a wrong thing to do. She also saw an angry little boy pulling a cat's tail. She told him not to, and he scowled at her. It was wicked to hurt animals, but was it wicked if a six-year-old did it? She wasn't sure. In an alley beside the boarded-up movie theater, she saw three teenage girls smoking. She wasn't sure about that one, either. Was it bad to smoke? Or only bad before a certain age? She would ask Mrs. Beeson.

For a few minutes, she followed along behind a group of kids to see if they were being cruel to each other, the way kids sometimes were. She saw some teasing, and a little roughhousing, but nothing much. She looked for Martin in this group, but he wasn't there.

When she was back where she had started, at the north end of Main Street, she headed downhill. The houses were farther apart here than in Greenhaven's neighborhood, and smaller. She saw a woman sitting on her front porch, reading the paper. A few children played ball in the street. No one was doing anything wrong, as far as she could tell. Really, Yonwood seemed like a very good town, so much better than dirty, crime-riddled Philadelphia. Following the words of the Prophet must be working.

Farther on, she came to what looked at first like a big, wild vacant lot. A high fence ran alongside it, and beyond the fence grew tall, unkempt trees. After a hundred yards or so, she came to a gravel drive with a mailbox beside it. "H. McCoy, 600 Raven Rd." was printed in black paint on the mailbox, and a "No Trespassing" sign was nailed to a tree. She recognized the name McCoy. Mrs. Beeson had mentioned this person. He was the one she was worried about, for some reason. She peered up the driveway. At the end, rising from a tangle of trees and rangy shrubs, she could just glimpse the peak of a roof. Tree branches threw shadows across it, and the shadows danced in the wind like long, thin ghosts. Should she go in there and see what H. McCoy was up to? Not today, she thought. Some other time. She walked on.

A block or so farther on, an alley led off Raven Road—really more of a wide path, rutted and unpaved. It went behind the houses on Trillium Street. Curious, Nickie turned that way.

From the alley, she could see into backyards. Most of them were empty and quiet. At one house she heard loud voices through an open window. She paused a moment to listen. The people inside were insulting each other and swearing. Surely that was bad. Did it mean they counted as sinners?

At the next house, a wire fence bordered the alley. Beyond the fence she could see the gnarled bare branches of fruit trees, and beyond those, the back of a house that badly needed a coat of paint. Just inside the fence, so close to the alley that she could have touched it if she'd wanted to, stood a shed made of weather-worn planks.

At this place, there was a lot going on. Two small children charged around among the tree trunks yelling at each other. One of them had a toy truck that the other seemed to want, and he chased his brother wildly, falling down on skids of slippery leaves, shrieking the whole time. A window in the back of the house opened, and an old woman stuck her head out and cried, "You kids quit that!" but the kids paid no attention.

Nickie watched them, peeking out from behind the shed so she wouldn't be noticed. The shrieking boy finally grabbed the truck away from the other boy, and that boy wailed furiously. Another child appeared, a girl maybe four or five years old, and scolded the boy who was crying. And then a bigger boy, closer to Nickie's age, burst out the back door. He had curly blond hair, big ears, and a strong, skinny body.

The boy leapt down the porch steps. "Hey, Roddie, lost your truck?" he called. "Want an airplane instead?" And he took hold of the little boy's hands and whirled him around so that he flew off the ground, squealing with laughter.

"Fly me!" said the other boy, and the big boy did. He flew the girl, too. Then he said, "Now, all of you quit making such a racket. There's plenty of toys inside. Go on."

"But I want—" the little boy started to wail.

"*Go on,*" said the big boy. "And leave me alone."

Nickie expected that he'd disappear back into the house, but instead he came toward the shed at the end of the yard. She ducked down quickly. He fiddled with the door for a moment—maybe it was locked, she couldn't see—and then opened it and went inside.

Nickie should probably have left at this point. She had no reason to think this was a trouble spot. But, as usual, curiosity took hold of her. What was the boy doing in this falling-down shed? Because the shed backed up against the fence, and because there was a dusty window in the back of the shed, just the right height for looking into, she might be able to see in without being noticed. She put her eye to the glass.

CHAPTER 12

Inside the Backyard Shed

It was Sunday morning and for once a sunny day. Grover's father was in the garage, getting ready to change the oil in the car. His mother had gone to church. Grover finally had some time to himself.

When the little kids had finished their breakfast, he shooed them outside. "Get out there and tear around," he said. "There's sun today, but it might be gone tomorrow." They charged into the backyard, and he sat with Granny Carrie at the kitchen table while she finished her cup of coffee. He contemplated his grandmother. She was wearing a plaid flannel shirt this morning, with an old green sweatshirt over it, and orange sweatpants with thick, fuzzy socks and her duck slippers. Her short white hair was so wispy that her pink scalp showed through.

"Going to sit out on the porch this morning," she said. "Take in some sun."

"You'd better wear a hat," Grover said. "It's chilly out there."

"I will," she said. "I've got that nice green-and-yellow one your mother knitted me."

Grover smiled to himself. His grandmother didn't care a bit what she looked like. She'd happily wear fifteen different colors, all clashing with each other. She sometimes looked like a heap of bright laundry with a little wrinkly walnut head on top. His mother was always trying to get her to spiff up, but Grover thought she looked fine the way she was: completely different from every other old lady in town.

From outside came five or six piercing shrieks. Granny Carrie rose from the table and hoisted up the window by the back door. "You kids quit that!" she yelled.

More shrieks followed, and then a wail.

"I'll go deal with them," Grover said. "I'm going out there anyway."

He took his jacket from its hook by the back door and went out into the yard. For a few minutes, he fooled around with the kids, and then he shooed them back into the house and went down to his shed. If the kids behaved, and if his father didn't call him to help with the car, he'd have at least an hour, maybe more, all to himself.

The shed's door was fastened with a combination lock, its combination known only to him. He twirled it, opened it, and went inside, closing the door behind him.

And as soon as he was in there, he became, as always, a different Grover. Not the funny Grover, not the big brother Grover, but the serious, brilliant, totally focused Grover, pursuing his passion.

A few rusted garden tools still hung on one wall of the shed, but he'd cleaned out all the old broken flower-pots and half-empty boxes of plant food and bags of moldy potting soil that used to be in here. Along one side of the shed he had built a wide shelf, and on the shelf were the two glass tanks, each equipped with lights and sitting on a heating pad, where he kept his prized possessions: his snakes.

He bent down and peered into each tank in turn. "How're you doing, my beauties?" he murmured. Both snakes were barely visible. They'd burrowed under the dry leaves and bark he'd put in the tanks for shelter. All he could see was a small patch of patterned scales pressed against the glass in one tank and the narrow tip of a tail lying across a twig in the other.

He checked the temperature in the tanks—86 degrees for one, 80 for the other. Just right. Then he raised the glass top of the tank on the left and set it down on the shelf. He reached inside in a slow, unstartling way, and he took hold of the snake gently, a few inches behind its head, and raised it up into the air.

It curved and whipped, looping itself into an *S*

and then a *J* and then an *S* again, flowing like a moving rope between Grover's hands. It was a gorgeous
creature, nearly two feet long. Rings of black and yellow and rusty red alternated all down its slim body. It
looked like a beaded belt, except that at the top end
was a head with glittering black eyes and a darting
tongue like a sliver of black paper.

"Pretty soon," said Grover, "I'll have some dinner
for you. Maybe tomorrow or the next day. Something
delicious." He held up the snake and looked it in the
eye. "Okay?"

This snake's name was Fang. He'd found it during
the summer, sleeping at the base of a rock in the
woods. It was the first milk snake he'd captured, and he
was very pleased with it. For nearly eight months now,
he'd kept it alive and healthy. Fortunately, it didn't have
to be fed very often during the winter. Finding food for
it wasn't easy, and he couldn't always afford to order
from the reptile supply company. Of the dozens of
snakes he'd captured in the last three years or so, he'd
kept this one the longest. If he couldn't find food for
his snakes, or if they started to look sickly, he always let
them go.

Grover was on his way to being a snake expert.
Four years ago, a snake had come out of the bushes
and crossed the path in front of him as he was walking
in the mountains. He had stopped and watched as it
slithered along, moving without legs, swimming with-

out water, a creature built all in one line, strange and beautiful and, to him, thrilling rather than frightening. He'd been nine years old at the time. The whole rest of that summer, he'd scrambled around in the woods, looking under rocks and logs and in holes in the ground, hoping to find a snake to take home with him so he could see it up close and watch it live its life. He went to the library and got out books about snakes, and on the library computer he went on the Internet and found endless pages of information and pictures. Before long his head was packed with snake knowledge.

For a while, he talked to everyone about this new passion—his parents, his grandmother, his friend Martin. But his parents were too busy to be very interested, and Martin didn't understand how he could care about such dirty, slimy things. Only his grandmother really listened. She thought it was a fine idea to collect snakes as long as he didn't ever show them to her. She said she would scream like a fire engine if any snake got close to her.

So now Grover kept his snakes to himself. He fixed up the shed (his father didn't have time for gardening anymore, so he didn't mind), and he used every penny he could earn on snake supplies. So far, he had found, kept, and released thirty-seven snakes. Only two had died in his care. He knew all the kinds of snakes around where he lived. Now his ambitions had grown.

He had a plan. All he needed to make it happen was money, and he was working on that. Success was near.

He told this to his snake. "Success is near, Fang," he said. "Really. No doubt about it. You'll see."

With the hand that wasn't holding Fang, he took the lid off the other tank. This tank held Licorice Whip, his young red belly snake. He'd had it only a few weeks. It was the thickness of a slender cord, about a foot long. He lifted it out. He held the two snakes up, one in each hand, and gazed at them as they wove among his fingers and coiled around his wrists, sliding their cool dry skin against his skin, raising their small, elegant heads and staring back at him, almost as if they were about to speak.

Then suddenly he heard a noise: a soft thump against the wall of the shed, and a rustling. He shifted his gaze to the dusty window just in time to see something move quickly on the other side. Someone was out there. As fast as he could, he set the snakes back in their tanks and put the lids on. Then he dashed out and ran along the fence to the gate that led out to the alley. Up ahead, going around the curve, someone was running, but it was too far away to see who. He didn't try to give chase. Probably it was Martin, who used to be his friend, trying to catch him doing something forbidden. He didn't bother to run after him. He went back to the shed.

"What is the *matter* with that guy?" he said to Fang and Licorice Whip. "Seems like he's out to get me."

He took Fang out of his tank, draped him around his shoulders, and started in on the task of cleaning tanks. But after he'd been working twenty minutes or so, he heard footsteps outside. The door of the shed opened, and his father leaned in. "Got an emergency job to do," he said. "Leaky pipe. I'm going to need your help."

Grover sighed. He put Fang back in his tank and, after locking up the shed, followed his father back to the house.

CHAPTER 13

The Perfect Living Room

Nickie had bumped against the shed by accident when her foot slipped on a stone. She'd seen the boy's face turned toward the window, and she'd dashed away, going up the hill toward town, running until she was sure no one was following her.

What she'd seen in the shed had given her a chill: the boy holding the snakes up in both hands and gazing at them so ardently, the snakes twisting in the dim air, their black tongues flicking in and out. She'd never seen a live snake before. Weren't most snakes poisonous? Wouldn't it be dangerous to have snakes in a place where there were little children? She felt a surge of excitement. This might truly be a trouble spot. She reminded herself of Mrs. Beeson's words: A sense of wrongness. Sometimes you can just *feel* it. The boy with the snakes definitely gave her a strange, creepy feeling. She walked faster. Mrs. Beeson would be home from church by now. She would go straight to her house. She had a lot to ask her about.

Mrs. Beeson's doorbell had three bell-like notes—*ting, ting, tong*. After Nickie rang it, she waited nervously. Maybe you were supposed to have an appointment to talk to Mrs. Beeson.

But the door opened, and there she was. She had no hat on, but she was still in her church outfit, and she had her DATT phone clapped up against her ear. Sausage came trotting up behind her and sniffed at Nickie's shoes.

"Just a sec, Ralph," Mrs. Beeson said into the phone. She smiled at Nickie. "Come on in, honey," she said. "I'll be off the phone in a jiff."

Nickie walked in. As she waited, she noticed again the round blue button pinned to Mrs. Beeson's sweater. What *was* that little picture on it? It seemed to be a tall, narrow building, like— Of course. It was a tower. And the Prophet's name was Althea Tower.

"So Ralph," Mrs. Beeson said into the phone, "you just have to trust me on this. We have to get everyone behind us, and if we need to use unusual measures, well, then we do. These are unusual times." She paused. "I know, I know, but that's what she said. I'm sure. Uh-huh. All right. See you later." She set down her phone and turned to Nickie. "Come right in here," she said, leading the way into the living room.

Nickie was curious to see if Mrs. Beeson's house was as perfect on the inside as it was on the outside. It was. Mrs. Beeson had the coziest and neatest living room Nickie had ever seen. A fat white couch sat opposite fat blue armchairs. A coffee table held a plate of cookies and three books, neatly stacked, the top one black with gold letters on the front—probably a holy book of some sort. Three pictures hung on the walls: one was a beautiful scene of a mountain lake, one was a color photograph of Sausage, and one was a photograph of a freckle-faced young man in a soldier's uniform. "My husband," Mrs. Beeson said. "Killed twenty-two years ago in the Five Nation War, fighting against our enemies." A vase of artificial roses stood on the mantel and next to it a box in the shape of a heart. There was no mess at all. No sweaters draped over chair backs, no flopped-open magazines, no shoes left on the floor. No *stuff* scattered anywhere. It was just the opposite of Greenhaven.

A jingly tune was playing softly, but Nickie couldn't tell where it was coming from.

"Mrs. Beeson," she said. "I need to ask you about some things."

"Very good!" said Mrs. Beeson. "Have a seat. Help yourself to a cookie."

Nickie sat on the white couch. Mrs. Beeson was about to sit down across from her when suddenly a soft roar started up, and a little dome-shaped machine rolled into the room. Sausage skittered frantically and jumped onto Mrs. Beeson's lap.

"Don't mind the robot vacuum," said Mrs. Beeson. "Just lift up your feet when it comes close. It makes Sausage a bit nervous, but I think it's marvelous. I've programmed it to do the whole house every other day."

Nickie watched, fascinated, as the vacuum trundled back and forth across the floor. "It's cute," she said. She took a cookie from the plate.

"It is, isn't it?" said Mrs. Beeson. "I've found many of the new gadgets so helpful. Like my little DATT phone. It can take pictures, send e-mail, record TV, get instant news, identify poisonous substances, tell one fingerprint from another . . . all kinds of useful things. Now if it could just detect wrongdoing!" said Mrs. Beeson, laughing. "What a help that would be." She scratched Sausage's ears. "So. You have something to ask me?"

"Yes, I do." Nickie set down her half-eaten cookie and told Mrs. Beeson about the old shed and the boy with the snakes twining around his arms. "I wasn't sure if he would count as a sinner or not."

"Snakes?" said Mrs. Beeson. She lifted a foot as the robot vacuum rolled beside her chair. "Where was this?"

Nickie told her.

"Interesting," said Mrs. Beeson. "I've been reading a great deal of spiritual literature these last months, and I haven't come across one good word about snakes."

"Some other things, too, I wondered about," Nickie said. "Spitting on the sidewalk, and pulling a cat's tail, and smoking. I wasn't sure about the cat or the smoking. It was a little boy hurting the cat, and some teenagers in the park smoking." Mrs. Beeson nodded, frowning. "And some people were yelling in a house on Trillium Street," Nickie went on. "It sounded like a bad fight, but I didn't hear what it was about."

"What address?" Mrs. Beeson asked.

Nickie described the house. "*And*," she said, suddenly inspired, "you know that man Hoyt McCoy?"

Mrs. Beeson leaned forward. The vacuum had moved on to another room now, so she set Sausage back down on the floor. "Yes? What about him?"

"When I passed his house," Nickie said, "I kind of peeked up the drive, and I saw strange shadows. Like black ghosts or something, hovering around outside. It made me feel creepy."

"Um-*hmmm*," said Mrs. Beeson. "Very interesting indeed."

"I know it was bad to spy," Nickie said. "And bad to eavesdrop, and to look in the window at the boy with the snakes. I probably shouldn't have done it, but—"

Mrs. Beeson held up a hand. She looked Nickie straight in the eye. For a moment she didn't speak, and

Nickie heard again the jingly tune that the noise of the vacuum had covered up. "You did well," Mrs. Beeson said. Her voice was solemn. "Listen, honey. I want you to remember this. When you know that you're doing God's work—then you're willing to do anything. I mean *anything*."

A shiver like a miniature lightning bolt shot through Nickie's middle, right beneath her ribs. *Anything* if it's God's work, she thought. Yes, that's what it is to be a holy person: you're willing to do anything. She thought of stories she'd heard about saints who let themselves be killed in awful ways. She thought about the brave characters in the books she loved, how they faced monsters and crossed flaming mountains and did not live by the rules of ordinary people. And it wasn't out of the question for someone as young as herself to be like them. Often, at least in books, it was a child who vanquished the darkness. She could be like that. She felt a great fierce desire to bring goodness to the world—or at least to Yonwood.

Mrs. Beeson stood up. Sausage got up, too. "What a help you are, honey," Mrs. Beeson said. "I think you and I have the same thing in mind—a bright, clean world where everyone knows how to behave! Wouldn't it be splendid?"

Nickie nodded, imagining it: everyone kind, everyone good, no creepiness, no wars.

"So the more of these trouble spots we can find,

the better off we'll be," Mrs. Beeson went on, her voice becoming very stern. "Remember what I said about how one moldy strawberry can ruin the whole basket? We're not going to let that happen. We're going to make this a good and godly town through and through." She bent over and swept the crumbs of Nickie's cookie into her hand. "And I'll tell you frankly, honey, I'm the one to get it done. I may look like a dumpling, but I have a spine of steel."

"Are you a preacher, Mrs. Beeson?" Nickie asked.

"No, no. I'm retired. But I can't just sit around, can I? That's not my way." She laughed. "I coach girls' baseball in the spring. I lead a study group at the church. Organize Yonwood's spring cleanup. Might even run for mayor someday. I like to wear a lot of different hats."

They headed for the hall, where several of Mrs. Beeson's different hats hung from a tree-shaped hat rack. "I keep hearing music," Nickie said. "Where's it coming from?"

"Oh!" said Mrs. Beeson, smiling. "It's my music box!" She darted back into the living room and picked up the heart-shaped box from the mantel. "It's very high-tech—powered by some new kind of tiny everlasting battery. Plutonium, I think. It just goes and goes. Isn't it charming?"

"Yes," said Nickie.

Mrs. Beeson opened the front door and ushered her out. "Thank you so much," she said. "Anything else you notice, you just come and let me know." She beamed at Nickie, and Nickie glowed.

Afterward, though, she felt a tiny bit guilty. She hadn't really seen ghosts hovering around Hoyt McCoy's house, or anything bad at all. She'd just had a *feeling* about the place. But everything else she'd said was true; maybe that made up for one small fib.

As she came through Greenhaven's front door, the telephone rang. She picked it up and said hello, and Amanda's voice answered. "Oh, good, it's you. I just remembered something. I still have the house key. I oughta bring it back."

"Okay," Nickie said. "Come whenever you want. And Amanda—anything new about the Prophet? Is she better?"

"No, she's just the same. Really sad and quiet. Keeps on saying stuff you can't figure out. Sometimes she wanders off."

"Wanders off?"

"Yeah, it's almost like she's walking in her sleep. She goes out in the yard, or even out the front door, and I have to quick go get her and bring her back."

"Is she trying to go somewhere?"

"I don't know."

"And I *still* can't come and meet her? Because I'm *so interested*, Amanda. Maybe *I* could tell what she's saying."

"I doubt it," said Amanda. "If Mrs. Beeson can't tell, I don't see how *you* could."

"Well, okay, maybe not," Nickie said. "But I'd like to just *see* her sometime. What does she look like?"

"She looks sick. All shadowy around the eyes." Amanda sounded impatient. "I have to go."

Nickie spent the next hour or so roaming around Greenhaven. She loved being alone here. She burrowed through the silent rooms like a miner hunting for gold. What she wanted was anything old, and especially anything written. From desk drawers and closet shelves and the backs of cabinets, and from the trunks and boxes in the third floor rooms, she pulled out packets of letters, programs from long-ago theater performances, journals and ledger books and guest lists and postcards. She sat on the floor reading until the air around her felt thick with the past. All these words, written so long ago, seemed to say to her, Remember us. We were here. We were real.

She kept Otis nearby. If she was sitting on the floor, he pushed his nose against her arm, wanting to be petted. He tugged at the leg of her pants, wanting to play. Sometimes he slept, stretched out, belly to the rug, his rear legs flopped behind him like a frog's. Now and then he would wander off, and when Nickie remembered to look for him, she'd find him chewing happily on the corner of a curtain, or trying to dig through the hardwood floor. He was all the company she needed.

Around two-thirty, when Crystal still wasn't back, she decided to take Otis for his afternoon outing. She heard banging as she went down the hall, probably coming from one of the bathrooms. The plumber must be here. She went out through the kitchen to the back garden.

To her surprise, the basement door was slightly ajar. The plumber must have gone down there to get at the pipes under the house. Good. She'd been curious about the basement—she could have a look. She picked Otis up, pulled open the door, and peeked in. The plumber had turned on the light. It was dim, just a bulb in the ceiling, but it showed her a flight of stone steps. Holding Otis tightly, she went down.

CHAPTER 14

Someone in the Basement

The basement was huge—a low-ceilinged room that stretched out into shadowy darkness ahead of her and to the left. It wasn't an empty darkness—she could see what appeared to be low hills lurking in the shadows. Another light bulb shone dimly in a far corner. Did that mean someone was down here? One of the workmen, maybe? She thought of calling out, "Anyone here?" But there was something still and heavy about the silence that made her afraid to break it. She would just look around a little, quietly, and then she would climb up the stairs and leave.

The air had a smell like the damp, earthy underside of rocks. Once her eyes had adjusted to the dimness, she saw that the hills were piles of furniture, a great crammed-together mass with just a narrow passage winding through it. Tables lay with their feet in the air, and between the feet were other tables, and dining room chairs and stools and chests of drawers, and on top of the chests were more chairs, upside down, making a nest for footstools and mirrors and lamp bases and unidentifiable things covered in sheets. Far back against the wall stood four-poster beds, some piled with three or four mattresses, and great looming wardrobes with mirrored doors. All of it had turned the same dirt-gray color because of the dust that coated it. Cobwebs drifted in long strings from the ceiling, brushing Nickie's face as she walked by. Otis squirmed in her arms.

She followed the passage that twisted through all this—it was like walking down a tunnel, almost, because the furniture was stacked shoulder-high. She moved toward the light.

She heard a scrape, and then a rustling sound.

She stopped, held her breath, and listened. Was someone in here? She bent down and peered through the forest of furniture legs, but it was too dark to see.

Something stirred over by the wall. Wood knocked against wood, a head rose from the jumble of furniture, and a voice spoke.

"Pa?" it said. "Is that you?"

"No," said Nickie. Her heart jumped, but curiosity kept her from running away.

The head ducked down again. There was more

scraping and rustling, and then someone crawled out from beneath a big table: a boy with cobwebs in his hair.

"I know who *you* are," the boy said. He held his hands cupped together as if protecting something. "The old guy's granddaughter."

"Great-granddaughter," said Nickie.

"And who's *that*?" He nodded at Otis, who was squirming in Nickie's arms.

"It's Otis," she said. "I'm taking care of him for somebody. Who are you?" She couldn't see the boy's face; the light was behind him. It cast his huge, blurry shadow onto a cabinet that leaned against the head-board of a bed.

"Grover," said the boy. "My pa is fixing your pipes."

"But what are you doing down here?"

The boy sprang toward her all of a sudden. "Lying in wait!" he cried. "For unwary creatures to fall into my trap!"

Nickie shrieked and then instantly regretted it, because he laughed to see that he'd scared her.

"I already caught one unwary creature," he said. He held up his clasped hands. "It's a prisoner now, awaiting its fate."

"What is it?"

He stepped toward her and she stepped back. She couldn't help it. He might have a spider in his hands, and he might be the kind of boy who would suddenly throw it at you.

"I'll show you if you're brave enough to look," he said. He stretched out his hands and opened them so she could see what he held. It was not a spider. She couldn't tell what it was. Something small and pinkish. Otis strained forward, sniffing madly. She put her hand around his muzzle.

"An infant mouse!" the boy cried. "There's eight of them in a nest down there by the heating pipe."

"Let me see," said Nickie. "Hold it in the light."

He did. It had hairless, almost transparent skin, tiny, twitching paws, and little blind eyes. It was about as big as a quarter. "Why did you steal it?" she asked him.

"I need it," he said. "For my snake."

"What?"

"For my snake to eat."

She looked up at the boy's face, which was framed in blond curly hair. His ears stuck out. She knew, suddenly, who he was.

"You don't believe me?" he said.

"I believe you," she said. "But I don't like it." She turned around and started back the way she'd come.

He followed her up the stairs and out of the basement. She set Otis down, and he sniffed Grover's shoes with great interest.

"Where'd the dog come from?" Grover asked.

"I'm just taking care of him for a little while," Nickie said. "He's a secret—don't tell about him, all right?"

Grover tilted his head upward and yelled, "Hey, everybody, guess what, there's a—"

Nickie shouted, "Stop it!"

He laughed. "I'll keep your secret," he said. "Now you owe me a favor."

"Are you really going to give that baby mouse to a snake?" Nickie asked.

"Yep." Grover stretched his mouth into a wicked grin. "Because I'm *meeean* and *eeeevil*," he said, and gave a maniac laugh. "Worse than"—he lowered his voice to a gruesome whisper—"Hoyt McCoy. Have you heard of him?"

Nickie nodded, feeling a lurch in her stomach.

"Well, I'm much worse than him," Grover said.

"You have spiderwebs in your hair," said Nickie. She turned and walked away from him, through the back door and into the house. What terrible luck, she thought. A boy right here where she could get to know him—and he turns out to be the boy with the snakes. And on top of that, a kidnapper and murderer of baby mice. She couldn't possibly fall in love with someone like him.

She went upstairs again, planning to read until Crystal got home. She switched on the lamp and picked up her great-grandfather's notebook. On the floor beside her, Otis went to sleep and dreamed, making soft little *wip-wip* noises and fluttering his paws. Nickie read:

> 1/2 Legs very weak and painful. Spent the day reading the scientific journals. Intrigued by this notion of extra dimensions—other worlds right next to ours? Had a chat with M but of course can't understand a word.

What might that mean? She knew about three dimensions—up, down, and sideways. What were extra dimensions? Who was M? She read on:

> 1/4 Extraordinary experience last night: Went into the back bedroom to look for the scissors, thought I saw someone in there, over by the bed—dark-haired figure, transparent swirl of skirt. Dreadful feeling of sorrow hit me like a wave. Had to grab the doorknob, almost fell. Figure faded, vanished. Maybe something wrong with my eyes. Or heart.

He was ninety-three when he died. Maybe he was losing his mind a little bit, thinking he was seeing ghosts. She read on:

1/19 Brenda B. came by today. All worked up, trying to figure out what Althea is saying and what to do about it. Kept talking about how she's studying every holy book she can get her hands on, aiming to understand God's word. I quoted St. Augustine to her: "If you understand it, it isn't God." Gave her a cup of chamomile tea.

That was interesting. But then came another mystifying one:

1/30 String theory—M theory?—eleven dimensions—gravity waves—alternate universes? Possible leakage between one universe and another? Amazing stuff. M says his research is very promising.

Maybe he thought he'd slipped into an alternate

universe in the back bedroom and seen a ghost, somehow. Which one was the back bedroom, anyhow? Nickie left the sleeping Otis and went down to the second floor, hoping to catch sight of the ghost herself. It was clear which one was the back bedroom: its window looked out over the backyard. She saw no ghost in that room, but through the window she saw Grover, who was probably waiting for his father. He was walking along the low wall that bordered the concrete terrace and crouching down every now and then to study the ground, maybe looking for more creatures to capture. She watched him for a minute. He was definitely good-looking. She liked the springy way he moved, and his floppy hair more or less covered up his sticking-out ears. She couldn't fall in love with him, of course, because of the snakes and the baby mouse, but she decided to go down and talk to him again anyhow.

When Grover saw her come outside, he beckoned to her, and she went over to him.

"Listen," he said, in an urgent whisper. "I want to show you something amazing. No human eye has ever lit on it before."

Nickie was wary. "Is it about snakes?"

"No, no," said Grover. "I told you, no one has ever seen this."

"Not even you?"

"Not even me."

"Well, what is it?" Nickie said.

Grover reached into his lunch bag and brought out a small green apple.

"I've seen apples before," Nickie said.

"Yeah, but watch this." Grover took out his pocket-knife, pulled the blade out, and sliced the apple in half across the middle. He pointed to the inside—the white flesh oozing juice, the five little seeds in a star shape.

"I've seen that, too," said Nickie.

"No, you haven't," Grover said. "No one has. Not a single person has ever seen the inside of this apple until now. It is a completely new sight to the human eye." He took a big bite out of one half of the apple and stood there chewing, with a wide, satisfied smile across his face.

"Oh, you think you're so clever," Nickie said. She grabbed the other half of the apple out of his hand. She was annoyed at being tricked, but she couldn't help smiling a little, too. What he'd said was true, after all.

An idea popped into her head. "I know something *you've* never seen before," she said. "No human eye has ever seen it, or ever *will* see it."

"That doesn't make sense," said Grover, munching on his apple.

"Yes, it does. I'll show you."

"But if you show me, then I will have seen it."

"No, you won't," said Nickie. "Just wait here. I'll go get it." She ran inside, went to her bedroom, and came back out clutching a piece of paper. She held it out. "Do you know what this is?"

Grover peered at it. "It's some fake monster out of a science-fiction movie," he said.

"Nope," said Nickie. "It's a dust mite. In this picture, it's magnified many, many zillion times. You will never see it in real life, because it's smaller than the eye can see."

"Hah," said Grover. He looked up at her and quirked an eyebrow. "Where'd you get it?"

"I cut it out of a magazine. I like strange, interesting things."

"You don't like snakes, though," Grover said. "Probably you're afraid of them."

"I am not."

"You'd never want to see a snake eat a mouse."

"Maybe I would." As soon as she said this, she realized it was true. It would be a horrible thing to see, but interesting. And it might help her decide if there was something evil about this boy or not.

"Really?" Grover looked surprised.

"Really."

"I don't believe you. You're just saying that to sound big."

This was somewhat true, but Nickie wasn't going to admit it. "Just tell me when," she said. "I'll come and see it."

So he said she should come the next day about three-thirty, and he told her how to get to his house. Just in time, she remembered not to say she already knew where he lived.

Crystal got back around five. She came in the front door, her cheeks red with cold and her eyes sparkling, talking and talking about the lovely scenery in the surrounding hills. "This really is a gorgeous area," she said. "I had *such* a wonderful time."

"Good," said Nickie, not really listening.

"And Len told me some interesting things about Yonwood," Crystal said. "A woman here has had some kind of religious experience, apparently. People think it means Yonwood is a sort of chosen place, and they'll be safe even if there's war."

Nickie started paying closer attention. "Does Len think that?"

"He doesn't know what to think," Crystal said, flinging her coat on a chair. "He was in school with this Prophet person. She was a shy, bookish little girl, he said, not the type to grab for attention. So he thinks maybe what happened to her was real. Have you heard anything about it?"

"A little," Nickie said, trying to look uninterested.

"Tomorrow," said Crystal, "I'm going to have my hair done at the local beauty shop. I'll probably come out looking like a dandelion, but at least that'll be better than *this* mess." She swatted at her bangs.

"Good idea," said Nickie, though she thought Crystal looked fine as she was.

"After that," Crystal went on, "I'm going into Asheville for some shopping. I don't suppose you want to come."

"No," Nickie said. "I don't want to come."

"What are you going to do?"

"Oh, nothing much," Nickie said. She didn't think it was a good idea to mention snakes or mice.

"You're such a good girl," Crystal said. "All this time on your own, and you never get bored or get into trouble. It's amazing."

Nickie just smiled.

CHAPTER 15

Up to the Woods

A few times during the next day, which was Monday, Grover found himself thinking about Nickie as he sat in his desk at school. He wasn't thinking about her in a boy-girl sort of way. The notion of "being in love" never entered his mind. He was thinking about her in an interesting-person sort of way. It wasn't often that he met anybody, especially a girl, who cared about things like dust mites. He was looking forward to showing her his snakes later on, after school. It would be fun to see if she was scared after all.

But first he had to do some hunting. Just before two o'clock, he filled in the last answers on his English test and then staged a highly realistic coughing fit. "Can't breathe! Nurse's office!" he gasped, and he staggered, choking, out of the classroom. Then he slipped out a side door and trotted up Fern Street to the path that led into the woods.

The forest was his second home. He knew all the trails that threaded up the mountainside. He knew the creeks and the outcroppings of rock and the places where salamanders were likely to be hiding under rotting logs. In the summer, he spent hours up here. Sometimes he scrambled through brush and waded down streams, but other times he just found a good spot and sat still. He had learned that if he sat without moving for a long time, he would see things. Animals would come out from their hiding places and potter around in the open, not realizing he was there. Once, at dusk on a summer evening, a spotted skunk walked past him, so close he could see the long, curved nails on its front feet.

Today he was after some dinner for his red belly snake. The milk snake would get the baby mouse, which he was trying to keep alive so that Nickie could watch it being eaten. For the red belly, a few good-sized slugs and maybe a small salamander would do. Actually, he could get these in his own backyard pretty easily. But he *wanted* to go into the woods. He hadn't been for a while, because of homework and bad weather and working on jobs with his father. He missed it.

He was aware that people had been talking lately about someone lurking up there, maybe a terrorist planning dark deeds. But Grover wasn't worried about him. He didn't think about him much. Talk about terrorists and war was the sort of talk that just slid off his brain. He was too occupied with his own concerns to pay much attention to it.

He started along a steep uphill trail, which would take him, in fifteen minutes or so, to a place where a stream rushed between shallow banks. He could get down to the water's edge easily there and find a few of the things that liked living in damp places. He'd brought a plastic jar with him to take them home in.

The rhythm of his steps said, Happy to be here, happy to be here. Rays of sunlight shot between the clouds, making spots of light like polka dots on the ground. On either side, the woods were thick—everything close in, dense, stickery, twined with vines, here and there a bare-twigged mountain ash with red berries like decorations. The whirr of bird wings rushed up from bushes as he passed. He was always looking beside the trail, which grew narrower as he climbed higher, for the holes and burrows that an animal might be living in. Holes, rotting logs, sun-warmed rocks—all those were places favored by snakes and therefore favored by Grover.

As he walked, he hummed a little tune—an ambling, careless tune that went with being happy and trotting along and knowing what he was doing—and his eyes scanned the woods and the ground for anything of interest, and his mind traveled off where it usually did, to his plan to join the Arrowhead

Wilderness Reptile Expedition this summer. It was perfect for him—Addison Pugh, a famous herpetologist, was leading it, and it was out in Arizona, where he'd never been and where the snakes would be all different from the ones here. He would have a great time, he would learn a huge amount, and he would meet people who could help him on the way to his career. He had to go. How could something as trivial as $375 stand in the way? It was very inconvenient that his family didn't have any spare money. On the other hand, it had forced him to be creative. He felt pretty confident about the cereal jingle he'd made up, and he'd solved the cryptogram and sent it in quickly. Sweepstakes weren't so promising, because winning was just luck. But he'd entered so many of them—at least fifty just in the last few weeks—that he *had* to win something. It wouldn't take much—just a few small prizes from three or four different contests, and he'd have enough.

All these thoughts swirling through his mind kept him a little less observant than he usually was. He was up fairly high on the mountainside now, and the trail turned into more of a dotted line up here, blocked every now and then by overgrown bushes or a fallen tree. This didn't matter to Grover. He climbed over or went around whatever was in the way; he always knew where he was. But it meant he had to watch his feet more, stepping over stuff and being careful not to trip, so at first he didn't see that something was moving farther up the mountainside, where the trees were denser. The sound of his own footsteps covered up the sound that anyone else's footsteps might have made. A few yards farther on, he came to the place where a muddy path led down the stream bank to the place he wanted to go, and there he paused for a second. That was when he heard a distant rustling, the sort of rustling that only something big makes.

He froze. Without moving any other part of himself, he turned his head toward where the sound seemed to have come from. The trees and the thick undergrowth beneath them made it impossible to see very far, or at least to see clearly. All he could see was a patch of paleness far off in the distance. It moved, paused, moved again, and disappeared. He stood still for another three or four minutes, but he heard no more rustling and saw nothing, either. So he went on down the stream bank and sat on a rock by the water.

Nothing large and pale lived in the woods, as far as he knew. He couldn't think what it could possibly be. Maybe some huge white bird? A stork? But why would there be a stork in the woods? There wouldn't. A ghost? He didn't believe in ghosts. Anyway, a ghost wouldn't make a rustling sound, would it?

So maybe the talk about someone lurking up here was worth paying attention to after all. Grover felt a small shiver of fear. Maybe this terrorist was up here just waiting for someone to kidnap. Give me a million dollars to fund my terrorist organization, or else I'll slice this boy up and scatter him in the pines.

Grover put his arms across his knees and hunched down, bending his face toward the water. The stream rushed by, carrying leaves and bits of twig, making the weeds at the water's edge flow sideways. He stayed that way for a while, imagining what he would do if a terrorist stepped suddenly from behind a tree and grabbed him. The best thing would be to have a snake with him at the time, so he could terrify the terrorist with it and startle him into letting go. A venomous snake would be best. If he didn't happen to have a snake, he'd have to struggle. Too bad he didn't know karate or any of those other martial arts. He could kick, though. He was strong and agile, and he could bite. He pictured himself twisting like a giant boa constrictor around the terrorist and biting him in the back of the neck.

It would be best, though, not to get caught in the first place. So he got busy with what he'd come for. He turned over rocks, dug the toe of his shoe into crumbling logs, lifted up sodden leaf litter, and poked sticks into holes. Before long he had some nice grubs, a millipede, five water snails, two good-sized slugs, and a small purplish salamander with gold spots on its back. He put these all in his jar and started down the trail.

CHAPTER 16

The Snake's Dinner

Shortly before three-thirty, Nickie set out for Grover's house. She'd seen it from the back—at least a glimpse of it beyond the shed and the fruit trees—but now she saw the front for the first time. It was a one-story yellow house with two battered tricycles standing out in the yard and three saggy steps leading up to a porch. On the porch was a couch covered in green material worn almost to white on the seat and arms, and on the couch sat a very old woman wearing a red housedress with a zipper up the front and a baggy lavender sweater. As Nickie came up the walk, the old woman peered at her.

"You're not from here," she said.

"No," said Nickie. "I'm just visiting."

The old woman nodded. She was wearing, Nickie noticed, yellow bedroom slippers with ducks on the toes.

"I'm looking for Grover," Nickie said.

But Grover must have seen her coming. The door opened, and there he was. "You *did* come," he said. "Amazing."

"Got yourself a girlfriend," the old woman said to Grover.

"She isn't my *girlfriend*, Granny," Grover said. "Just a girl."

Inside, the house was dim and crowded. The TV was on—it was the president, announcing that only four days remained before the deadline he'd set for the Phalanx Nations. But no one was paying attention. The living room was full of sagging furniture, and every piece of furniture seemed to have a child climbing on it, or curled up in it, or crawling out from under it. They all stared at Nickie when she came in.

"My brothers and sisters," Grover said, waving a hand at them.

"How many are there?" Nickie asked, spotting another one toddling up the hall.

"Six. The twins and four more. Plus me—I'm the oldest."

He led her down a short hall that went right through the house. The walls were covered with photographs—school pictures, wedding pictures, baby pictures, some in frames and some stuck up with thumbtacks.

They went out the back door, and Grover led the

way across the sloping yard, over the dead grass and brown rain-plastered leaves, between the gnarled trunks of the fruit trees, down to the shed beside the alley.

Nickie began to feel nervous. Her stomach clenched.

Grover twirled the dial of a combination lock on the latch and opened the shed door. She followed him in. The air had an earthy smell. A few garden tools, mostly broken, hung on hooks on the walls. On a shelf across one wall were the two snake tanks, and on other shelves, and on the floor, and on a small table and a chair were piles and piles of magazines and flattened cereal boxes, soap boxes, and cake mix boxes. The whole mess was sprinkled here and there with little bits of bent cardboard.

"What's all that?" Nickie asked.

"Contests," said Grover. "Sweepstakes, lottery tickets, stuff like that. There's gobs of dollars out there being given away. I enter everything I can find."

"Why?"

"Because I need money, *obviously.*" He made a "how can you be such a moron" face at her. "I want to go on the Arrowhead Wilderness Reptile Expedition this summer, which costs three hundred seventy-five dollars, which I don't have. So I'm going to win it."

"People hardly ever win contests," Nickie said. "I don't know anyone who has."

"Well, you will pretty soon," Grover said. "Look at

this one." He held up a page torn from a magazine. "You write one paragraph, no more than a hundred words, saying why Armstrong Pickles are the best. Want to hear my paragraph?"

"Okay," said Nickie. She glanced uneasily at the two glass tanks on the shelf, but she didn't see anything inside, only dry leaves.

Grover rummaged around on the table and came up with a sheet of binder paper. He read: "Last Sunday night, I was studying for my math test. It was late, and I was tired. My eyes kept closing so I couldn't see the numbers in my book. I thought, How am I going to pass this test if I can't stay awake? Then inspiration hit me. I needed an Armstrong Pickle! I jumped up from my chair and ran to the refrigerator. I pulled one of those big, green, pimply pickles out of the jar. The first cool bite made my brain go ZING! And the next day I got an A on the test." Grover looked up, grinning. "Only ninety-eight words."

Nickie laughed. "It's great," she said. "What do you get if you win?"

"You get five hundred dollars plus a whole free crate of pickles," said Grover. "There's all kinds of contests. Ones where you think up a slogan, and ones where you make as many words as you can out of some product's name, and ones where you solve a cryptogram, and—"

"Have you won any of them yet?" Nickie asked.

"Oh, yeah," said Grover. "I won six free boxes of Oat Crinklies, and I won a bunch of coupons for Rosepetal laundry soap. Just no money yet, but that will come."

He turned to the snakes. "All right," he said. "Time to get down to business. First the milk snake. He hasn't eaten for a few weeks."

"A few *weeks*!"

"Yep. They don't eat much in the winter. Snakes out in the wild around here crawl down underground and hardly eat at all till spring. Hey, you know what I saw when I was up in the mountains looking for snake food?"

"What?"

"I saw that terrorist. The one who broke the restaurant window."

"You *did*? Weren't you scared?"

"Nah. He was far away. Big, though. Huge. I just caught a glimpse of him."

Grover took the top off one of the tanks. Inside it, the snake stirred, lifting its head and then more and more of itself from the bark and dry leaves that covered it. Rings of black, yellow, and reddish-brown striped its long body.

"It doesn't look a bit like milk," Nickie said.

"I know it," said Grover, gazing fondly at the snake. "It's called that because people used to find them in their barns and think they'd come to milk the cows."

From a small cardboard box next to the snake tank, he took out the tiny mouse he'd shown Nickie before. It was pink and wet-looking, with a tiny head and bulgy bluish eyes, and tiny legs with tiny toes like fringe at the ends. It was moving slightly in Grover's palm, but it looked limp and weak.

"Bye-bye, baby," Grover said. He picked up a long pair of tongs, the kind people use to turn meat on a barbecue grill. His teasing manner was gone now. He moved carefully. All his attention was on what he was doing. He gripped the tiny mouse with the tongs and waved it back and forth before the snake's head. The snake lifted the front half of its body into the air. Its tongue flicked in and out.

"I don't know," said Nickie. "Maybe I don't want to watch."

But it was too late. The snake struck out and snatched the mouse. It withdrew into the tank and wrapped a coil of itself around the mouse's body to hold it still, and then it opened its mouth extremely wide and began to stuff the mouse's head into it.

"They always eat things headfirst," Grover remarked. "And they have expandable jaws."

Nickie froze in horror, but she couldn't take her eyes away. It took only a few seconds for the pink body of the mouse, still wriggling, to disappear down the snake's throat. For a second, a bit of tail hung over the snake's lower jaw. Then the whole mouse was gone. The snake stretched out on the sand again. Behind its head was a mouse-sized bulge.

Nickie breathed out. She hadn't realized she'd been holding her breath. She felt ill. "It's horrible," she said.

"Not really," said Grover. "It's how the snake lives. If I didn't give him a mouse, he'd catch one himself."

"How can you stand to do it? The poor little mouse."

Grover shrugged. "It's nature," he said. "Nature likes the snake just as much as the mouse."

"I guess so," Nickie said.

"Well, that's it," said Grover. He set down the tongs and put the lid back on the tank. "At least you didn't faint."

"I've *never* fainted," said Nickie. She felt upset— somewhere between sick and angry.

"Want to see the red belly eat?"

"No. It's too weird."

"It's not weird at all," Grover retorted. "It happens every day, hundreds of times. If you want to see something *really* weird, go over to Hoyt McCoy's house in the middle of the night. He cracks the sky open. I saw it."

"Come on," said Nickie. "You're making that up."

"No! I really saw it. A long, skinny line in the sky. He's doing *something* weird over there. Maybe he's sending signals to enemy nations! Or he opens the sky, and aliens and demons ooze through!" Grover wiggled his fingers in a creepy, oozing way.

Nickie just shook her head. With Grover, she didn't know how to tell the difference between truth and kidding. "I have to go now," she said. So Grover led her back across the yard and into the house, down the hall among the toddlers, and out onto the front porch, where the grandmother was still sitting on the old couch.

"Going already?" the old woman said.

"I showed her the milk snake," said Grover.

"No wonder she's leaving in a hurry."

"Fed him his dinner," said Grover.

"It was gruesome," Nickie said.

"No kidding," said the grandma. She eyed Nickie with interest. "You going to introduce me to this young lady?" she asked Grover.

"This is my grandmother, Carrie Hartwell," Grover said to Nickie. "We just call her Granny Carrie." He turned to his grandmother. "And this is Nickie," he said.

"Nickie Randolph," said Nickie. "My great-grandfather lived here. His name was Arthur Green."

"Ah," the grandmother said. "He was on the side of the angels."

Nickie wasn't sure what this meant, but it sounded all right. She said goodbye and walked back out to the street. Her legs felt shaky and her stomach churned. Was it good, she wondered, to feed a baby mouse to a snake? It wasn't good for the mouse, but it was for the snake. Was it evil for Grover to do it? She just didn't know.

CHAPTER 17

Hoyt McCoy's Horrible House

Nickie headed back toward Greenhaven by way of Raven Road. She hadn't really planned to go that way; her mind was on what she'd just seen in Grover's shed. But when she found herself passing the gravel drive that led back into Hoyt McCoy's overgrown acres, she hesitated. She thought about what Grover had said—that Hoyt McCoy cracked open the sky. Surely that couldn't be true. But whatever he'd seen might have been a sign of wickedness. Mrs. Beeson thought there was something strange about this man, that he was probably a trouble spot. And Nickie had promised to help her. So maybe, while she was here, she should check on Hoyt McCoy. She didn't really want to; even her strong curiosity didn't extend to creepy isolated houses and people with a whiff of wrongness about them. But if she was going to do her part to root out badness so that goodness could win, she had to be brave.

She gritted her teeth and took a deep, shaky breath. She would just dart in and have a quick look around, hoping to see something that would let her take back a clear report to Mrs. Beeson.

She started up the driveway. Brown, shriveled blackberry vines grew along the edges; weeds sprouted up through the gravel. Tall pine trees on the left cast a spiky line of shadows, and Nickie stayed within these shadows as much as she could. She rounded a curve, and there, up ahead, was the house, a mud-colored two-story building tucked back among great looming oaks and pines, its paint worn off, drifts of old leaves on its peaked roof. She stopped and looked for signs of movement. Three birds shot up from a clump of grass, but other than that, she saw nothing stirring, either outside the house or behind its windows. So, cautiously, she moved forward again.

What was she looking for? She didn't really know. Something truly awful, like freshly dug graves or human bones? Signs of craziness, like Hoyt McCoy dancing around naked? Disgusting filthiness, like a smelly outhouse or rat-swarmed garbage? She didn't see anything like that—nothing but a dusty black car parked at the head of the drive. Maybe bad things happened inside that dark, silent house, but she certainly wasn't going to go close enough to peer in the windows. She would go up to the beginning of the brick path that led to the front door, she decided, and if she didn't see anything notable by then, she'd leave.

So she crept away from the protective shadow of the trees and tiptoed across the open space in front of the house. She stood at the foot of the path. Her gaze scanned the front door, the windows to the left and right of the front door (heavily curtained), the windows on the second floor (where the blinds were closed), and a window in a gable above them, where—she took a sudden step backward, and her knees went weak—the barrel of a gun pointed at the sky.

And as she stood there, frozen with fear, the gun angled downward until it aimed straight at her. From inside the house, a voice called out, "Stop right there, trespasser, intruder, spy! Don't move, on pain of dire consequences!"

But Nickie was not going to stand there and get shot. She dashed toward the shadow of the trees as fast as her jelly-like legs would carry her. Any second, she expected to hear a bang and feel the punch of a shot between her shoulder blades. At the edge of the driveway she stumbled and fell, and she lay there for a second, shaking, and looked back at the house. The gun was still pointing downward, but no one was shouting; no one was coming out the front door. So she staggered to her feet again. This time her legs worked, and she ran.

She knew Crystal wouldn't be home yet. So she ran straight to Mrs. Beeson's house, leapt up the steps, and rang the doorbell. When Mrs. Beeson answered, Nickie was breathing so hard she could barely speak. "Mrs. Beeson!" she gasped. "That McCoy man tried to shoot me!"

Mrs. Beeson's eyes grew so wide that the whites showed all the way around. "What? Shoot you!"

Nickie told about the gun pointing out of the window and the voice that had bellowed at her.

"Oh!" Mrs. Beeson grasped Nickie by the arm and pulled her inside. "This is even worse than I thought. I must get the police—must get them out there right now—" She hurried away down the hall, leaving Nickie quivering by the door. In a moment Nickie heard her speaking to someone on the phone. "Raven Road," she said. "Yes, McCoy. Be careful—he has guns. I'll meet you out there."

When she came back, she was pulling on her coat. "We'll bring him in," she said. "Don't worry. You poor, brave little thing." She gave Nickie a quick, sweet-smelling hug. "I should have known—that feeling I had. Why didn't I—?" She clasped her hands and took a deep breath. "Slow down, Brenda," she told herself. "Be calm."

But Nickie wasn't calm at all; she was terribly excited. "There's more!" she said. "The boy with the

snakes—he feeds them live baby mice! And that terrorist up in the woods—he saw him! And he told me that
Hoyt McCoy cracks the sky open and sends signals to
enemy nations!"

Mrs. Beeson snatched her purse from a table by
the door. "I have to get out there right away," she said.
"You go back home now and keep yourself safe. Who
knows, he might be—But we'll get him, don't worry.
I'll come and talk to you when it's all over."

Nickie went back to Greenhaven wishing, for once,
that Crystal was around so she could tell her about
what had happened. But the only sign of Crystal was a
note she'd left on the hall table by the phone:

Nickie—

Your mom called. Sounded pretty tired and worried.
Another postcard came from your dad. It said:

Dear Nickie and Rachel,

Everything here is going well. We're working hard
and making good progress. I hope both of you are
taking excellent care of yourselves.

Love, Dad

P.S. Stayed up till midnight last night reading

Shakespeare!

I didn't know your dad read Shakespeare.

Back by dinnertime—C.

I didn't know he did, either, Nickie thought. There was something odd about these postcards. She needed to think about them. Was he trying to send a message of some kind? He'd always liked codes and puzzles. He'd explained a lot of different ones to Nickie, and they'd had fun working on them together. Could these postcards be in code?

She went up to the nursery and laid the three postcard messages in a row on the window seat. She studied them for a while, but if they were in code, she couldn't figure it out. So she gave up for the moment and played with Otis for a long time. His happy spirit made her feel better. Everything about him made her feel better, in fact—his damp black nose, the way the wavy hair grew on the top of his head, the five little pads on the bottoms of his feet, even his doggy smell. They played all their favorite games, and Nickie pondered her father's odd messages, and thoughts of horrible Hoyt McCoy gradually faded from her mind.

CHAPTER 18

What Grover Saw

Something was going on at Hoyt McCoy's. Grover, who was out by the street getting the mail just before dinnertime, saw two cars—one of them a police car— streaking down Trillium Street and veering left up Raven Road, and of course he followed to see where they were going. They turned in at Hoyt's driveway. Obviously they weren't just stopping for a friendly visit. They were going fast. Their wheels skidded on the driveway's gravel.

Had Hoyt had a heart attack or something? Had he maybe shot himself in the foot with that rifle of his? Maybe he had shot someone else and they were going in to arrest him. Whatever was happening, Grover had to see it.

He ran up Hoyt's driveway in the wake of the cars and stepped in among some trees at the side of the drive so he could watch without being seen. Both cars had pulled up in the open space in front of Hoyt's awful-looking house, and from them sprang Yonwood's policemen and Mrs. Brenda Beeson. The cops had taken their guns from their holsters and were pointing them at the front door of the house. The chief, Officer Gurney, roared in his chest-deep voice, "Hoyt McCoy! Come out with your hands up! We have you surrounded!"

Actually, they didn't have him surrounded. They were all in front of the house. But when Gurney said that, a couple of police scurried around to the back. Mrs. Beeson, in her red baseball cap, stood behind the other two. Her fists were clenched at her sides, her nose slightly wrinkled, as if she were sniffing the air, and her eyes fixed like searchlight beams on the front door of the house.

In a moment, the door opened. The tall, stooped figure of Hoyt McCoy appeared. He had on a baggy olive green sweater and black pants, and his shaggy hair stuck together in bunches, as if he hadn't combed it for several weeks.

"Hands up! Hands up!" yelled Officer Gurney, who must have learned his lines, Grover thought, from watching cop shows on TV.

But Hoyt did not put his hands up. He came out onto his front step and stared at the crowd in his driveway as if he thought he must be having a nightmare. Then he raised one hand, but not in surrender. He pointed a finger straight at Officer Gurney. "Off . . . my . . . property!" he shouted. "All of you. *Out!* What do you think you're doing here?"

"You're under arrest!" yelled Officer Gurney, though he didn't take a step closer to Hoyt. "Attempted murder!"

At this, Hoyt lowered his arm and smiled. Smiled? Grover crept a little closer to make sure. Yes, he was smiling, a strange look on that long, bloodhound face of his. He smiled and shook his head slowly. He came down his front steps and approached Officer Gurney, apparently not worried that he was about to be shot. Gurney raised his other arm and took hold of his gun with both hands, as if a tank or an enraged rhinoceros were charging at him.

"Officer," said Hoyt, "a mistake has been made, and I see the source of it standing just behind you." He nodded at Mrs. Beeson, who didn't move. "For some reason, this lady is determined to *hound* me. She sends her spies to trespass on my land. Now she accuses me of murder, which is so ludicrous that I can only smile." He smiled again, a thin, grim smile that had no humor in it.

Mrs. Beeson stepped forward, and Grover stepped forward, too, to hear what she was going to say. It didn't seem to matter if he came out a little from among the trees; no one was paying any attention to him.

"*Attempted* murder," Mrs. Beeson said in a voice that quivered with outrage. "I have always known that you were a bad one. But now we have found you out before you could—"

"Attempted murder of *whom,* madam?" said Hoyt.

"A child! A little girl who had strayed onto your land and was perfectly innocently gazing at your dreadful—"

"Now, wait just a moment, dear lady," Hoyt said. His smile vanished. His face grew dark with anger. "This is really too much! Lately my estate has been *crawling* with prowlers. A boy, a girl, and no doubt others I have not spotted."

Grover knew who the boy prowler had been. But who was the girl? He didn't know any girls who would even think of setting foot on Hoyt McCoy's land.

Hoyt railed on. "*Why,* a person would like to know? *Why?* I happen to be intensely busy at the moment—busy with matters of great importance, matters that could alter the world's future—and yours, madam. And yet you send spies to pester me." He shook his finger at Mrs. Beeson. "And when I call out at them, when I rightfully demand that they leave the premises, I am accused of attempted *murder*? It is quite beyond belief."

All this time, the police remained in a half-crouching position, like runners at the start of a race, ready at any second to leap forward and wrestle Hoyt McCoy to the ground. Hoyt didn't seem to be alarmed by this. He glared straight past them and fixed his eyes on Mrs. Beeson.

She glared back. "You trained a rifle on a little girl," said Mrs. Beeson in a breathless, furious voice. "A *rifle*. She saw it, and she saw you lower it—to point straight at her! She heard you—you threatened her. You—" Here she seemed to run out of both words and breath. Her face was as red as her cap.

Officer Gurney took a bold stride forward. "Come quietly now," he said to Hoyt. "We're taking you in."

But an expression of great amusement slowly spread across Hoyt's face. "Ah," he said, ignoring Gurney. "Now I understand. Look up there, ladies and gentlemen." He pointed upward and backward, over his shoulder. "There's your murder weapon."

Grover looked up. So did the cops, and so did Mrs. Beeson. In a gable window above the second story, the barrel of a rifle pointed at the sky. At least, it looked to Grover like a rifle, although it was bigger than the rifle his father had, and its shape was slightly different. Maybe it was actually a shotgun. That would explain why it was pointed at the sky—Hoyt was using it to shoot birds, when he wasn't shooting trespassers.

"That," said Hoyt, "is not a gun. That is the telescope with which I scan the skies." He turned back to glare at Mrs. Beeson again. "And also scan my property for trespassers. I wish to be left alone. But you, Brenda Beeson, send one spy after another. Why? *Why?* Why cannot a person be left in peace?"

It was an interesting moment. Grover held his breath, waiting to hear what Mrs. Beeson and her men would say. Everyone waited. Mrs. Beeson, too, seemed to be waiting, perhaps for a cue from God. Grover could see her face tightening—eyes narrowing, forehead furrowing. Really, he thought, she ought to be relieved. She ought to be saying, Oh, good, no crime has taken place after all! My mistake! Very sorry!

Instead she told Officer Gurney to take one of his men and go upstairs to make sure that Hoyt McCoy was telling the truth. "And look around as you go," she added. "In case—you know—there might be—"

"Absolutely," said Officer Gurney.

"What!" cried Hoyt. "You assume you may come barging into my house without a search warrant?"

"It's a matter of security," Officer Gurney said. "In times like these, a threat to security changes the rules."

"Outrageous," said Hoyt. "But I won't take the trouble to stop you. You will find nothing in my house that has the faintest whiff of criminality."

He went inside with the two men, and they were gone for about fifteen minutes—a very boring fifteen minutes for Grover, who didn't want to draw attention to himself by walking away. The cold from the ground

was seeping up into his feet. Mrs. Beeson got into her
car and sat there waiting. She looked cross and hud-
dled, as if *she* were the suspect about to be taken in.
Grover thought this was rather funny. He didn't really
favor one side over the other in this dispute. He hadn't
enjoyed being yelled at and scared by Hoyt McCoy the
day he crossed his property. But he didn't care much
for Mrs. Beeson, either. These days she was seeing something wicked everywhere she looked.

The police came out of the house, finally, and
Hoyt stood on his step with his hands on his hips and
watched them triumphantly as they got back into their
car.

"Your timing was excellent," he said. "If you'd come
tomorrow, you'd not have found me here, as I am
about to go away for a few days on a mission of more
importance than you can imagine. You might have
tried to interfere with my trip, which would have been
a very bad decision. As it is, we've got this little matter
out of the way and I hope never to have the pleasure of
your company here again."

The men weren't bothering to listen to him. "Weird-
est place I've ever seen," Grover heard Officer Gurney
say before he slammed the car door. "Messiest, too.
The guy's a nutcase."

The cars started up their engines and drove off
down the driveway. Hoyt stood where he was, watching until both cars had turned onto Raven Road.

Grover waited for him to go back inside, but he kept standing there, and finally Grover realized that Hoyt was looking right at *him*.

"I see my trespasser is back," Hoyt said. There was no anger in his tone.

"I'm leaving," said Grover. "I just wanted to see what was going on."

"Since you're here," said Hoyt, "let me tell you something."

Uh-oh, thought Grover. Now I get yelled at. But he stood his ground. At least no one was shooting at him.

Hoyt came down the steps, stalked over to Grover, and stood right in front of him. There were grease stains on his sweater, Grover noticed, and his pants were unraveling at the cuffs. He smelled like burned toast. "What Lady Brenda doesn't know," Hoyt said, "is that she has the wrong information. Heaven is *my* territory. I know what goes on there. I know what the universe has in store for us."

"You do?" said Grover. Not being yelled at surprised him so much that he answered as if they were having a normal conversation.

"As well as anyone," said Hoyt.

"Well," said Grover, "what *does* the universe have in store?"

"Ceaseless marvels," said Hoyt McCoy. "Infinite astonishment. But only for those who care to pay attention."

"I saw a crack of light over your house," Grover said.

"Aha," said Hoyt. He narrowed his eyes and looked hard at Grover. "Never mind about *that*," he said.

"Why?" said Grover. "Is it a secret?"

Hoyt McCoy ignored his question. "If you were to simply ring my doorbell like a civilized person instead of sneaking around my property, I might show you a few things. Assuming you were interested."

But Grover wasn't nearly interested enough for that. "Maybe sometime," he said. "But right now I have to go." He moved backward a few steps.

"Let me tell you one more thing," said Hoyt, raising his voice. "You may tell this to your Mrs. Beeson, if you like, who likes everything to be neat and clean and normal. I am *not* particularly neat or clean; I am certainly *not* what anyone would call normal. But I am as *good* as anyone else."

And very loony, thought Grover. He murmured a few more polite words and made his exit, trotting down the gravel drive and heading home with a great sense of relief.

Grover couldn't sleep that night. Thoughts swarmed through his mind; he couldn't shut them off. So he got up, being quiet so he wouldn't wake his brothers. He put his clothes on and went outside. He would take a short, fast walk—just up the hill to Main Street, down a few blocks, and back home. He'd done it before when he couldn't sleep, and it usually helped.

He wasn't afraid. There was nothing in Yonwood that could hurt him, unless that terrorist was roaming around town again. And if he was, Grover could watch him from some safe place and see what he was up to and turn him in. The thought was invigorating. Grover started off. He climbed the hill at a rapid pace, breathing in cold night air, looking up at the stars, wondering why he didn't do this more often. Being out alone at night made him feel free.

He went up Trillium Street, around behind the Cozy Corner (no terrorists there tonight), and down Main Street, where the streetlamps were out, as they were all over town. He saw nothing stirring—not a night watchman or an alley cat or even a spider—until, as he passed the dark windows of the grocery store, he happened to glance up Grackle Street and saw someone about a block away. Whoever it was didn't walk purposefully but drifted a little this way, a little that way, as if lost or looking for something. Was it a sleepwalker? Grover stopped and stared. He was too far away to be sure who he was seeing, but suddenly he thought he knew. It must be her; it was the right street. Why would she be outside? She seemed to be wearing—what? A nightgown? Something pale and floaty. He started in that direction. But before he'd gone more than a few steps, another figure appeared, a skinny girl, who dashed up behind the lost-looking one and took her arm and led her back into the house.

Grover turned downhill and headed for home. What he'd seen had given him a sad, shaky feeling. Poor Prophet, he thought. It must be awful to have God speak to you and turn your mind to ashes.

CHAPTER 19

Blue Envelopes

Nickie woke on Tuesday morning to the sound of rain roaring on the roof and slashing against the window glass, coming in gusts as the wind blew one way and then another. It was the sort of day when you want to stay inside, make a fire, and sit by it with your cup of hot chocolate. But of course Nickie had given up hot chocolate, so she drank mint tea that morning instead. She actually felt quite virtuous doing it, because it was so hard. She could tell that her willpower was being exercised, like a muscle. This didn't make her *happy*, exactly. She missed the chocolate. But it made her feel strong. Could it be that the more things you gave up, the stronger you would feel?

Crystal went out early to talk with Len about plans for the open house. "Meet me at the café at six," she said as she went out the door. "We'll have dinner together and you can tell me all about your adventures."

Otis's outing was very short that morning. He stood on the threshold of the back door and looked doubtfully at the rain. Nickie had to push him outside. Once there, he did his duty in record time and dashed back in. Nickie took him upstairs.

The nursery room was especially cozy that morning, with the sky so dark outside, and the sound of the rain on the windows, and the pools of golden light from the lamps. Nickie set Otis up on the window seat and gave him a new bone to chew. She propped up some cushions to lean against, and then she looked around for something to read. Her eyes fell on the books that Amanda had left behind. Why not try one of those? She picked the one with the dark-haired beauty on the cover and opened it at random:

In the candlelight, Blaine's eyes glittered like jewels. Clarissa caught her breath as he leaned toward her. What a magnificent man he was! His square jaw, his thick glossy black hair, his wide shoulders—her heart raced. When he reached out and stroked her cheek, she trembled all over. "Blaine," she said. "You must never leave me. I want to be with you always."

Nickie raised her eyes to the rain-spattered window. She tried to imagine feeling this way about someone. First she pictured Martin, with his hazel eyes and short red hair. Did she think he was magnificent? Not really. He seemed nice, and he was on the side of goodness. But he didn't make her heart race. She pictured Grover instead. His hair was cute, in a floppy sort of way. He was smart and interesting. He had a sense of humor, if you liked that kind of humor. But he was also a bit peculiar. She had no idea if he was on the side of goodness or not. And she certainly wouldn't say he was magnificent. If he stroked her cheek, would her heart race? No. She would think it was weird and creepy. Did she want to be with him always? Definitely not. It was hard to imagine wanting to be with anyone *always.* There'd be times when you wanted to be alone, or with someone else.

She turned a few pages and read some more:

Clarissa fled down the stone steps to the wind-swept beach, her raven tresses flowing out behind her. She scanned the empty sands, and when she saw no sign of Blaine, a great cry of anguish escaped her lips. She could not live without him! She would sooner die!

Nickie shut the book. There was no doubt about it: if that was love, she was not in love with Martin *or* Grover. She could live without either of them perfectly well.

She looked out the window, where the rain was still pelting down. At the end of the block, she noticed someone approaching, wearing a wide-brimmed pink rain hat and carrying a canvas tote bag. When the person came closer, she saw who it was: Mrs. Beeson! How perfect. If she ran fast downstairs, she could catch her and ask her what had happened to horrible Hoyt McCoy.

She didn't bother to grab an umbrella—she just threw on her jacket and ran out into the rain. Rivers of water streamed through the gutters. All along the street, bare tree branches flailed against house walls and shut-tight windows. She ran to meet Mrs. Beeson, who smiled when she saw Nickie coming.

"Hi!" said Nickie. "I saw you from the window, and I was wondering—"

"I was just thinking of you," Mrs. Beeson said. She looked a little frazzled around the edges. Her lipstick was slightly crooked, and her ponytail, beneath the rain hat, was damp and drooping. "You've been such a help. Walk with me, if you'd like. I'm delivering a few notices."

"Notices?" said Nickie.

"Yes, urgent ones. I'm getting a little impatient. Here we have such a miraculous chance to save ourselves, and a few people are about to ruin it for everyone. Such selfishness! I have to make them understand.

We have a terrorist in the woods! The Crisis gets worse all the time! In three days we might face war!" Mrs. Beeson shook her head at people's foolishness. "So I've decided it's time to take some drastic action. I've done the downhill ones and most of the uphill; only one more to go." She drew Nickie in next to her, under the umbrella. Her sugary smell enveloped them both.

"What are the notices about?" Nickie asked.

But Mrs. Beeson was already on a different subject. "It was just too bad about Hoyt McCoy," she said, "wasn't it? About your mistake, I mean, honey. But I still feel sure that he has something to hide. Don't you?"

Nickie was puzzled. "I don't *know* what happened with Hoyt McCoy," she said. "That's what I wanted to ask you. Didn't you arrest him? Did I make a mistake?"

Mrs. Beeson looked at her in surprise. "You didn't know?" She explained about the police action and the rifle that was really a telescope. "However," she said, "I'm sure we were right *essentially.* He just reeks of wrongness. I can *feel* it, and doing this work makes me trust my feelings more every day. It's just a matter of catching him in the act, that's all. But never mind. Here's the last house."

Nickie was so stunned by this news about Hoyt McCoy that she could hardly breathe. A telescope! And the police had gone out and aimed guns at him! Because of her.

They had stopped at a brick house with a collapsing woodshed next to it. Mrs. Beeson opened the mailbox. She reached into the canvas bag and took out a blue envelope. In the upper left corner were the words "Urgent: From B. Beeson." She put it in the mailbox, and they moved on.

Nickie started to ask again what was in the envelopes, but Mrs. Beeson was already talking. "Sometimes I'm sorry this ever happened," she said. "That vision of Althea's, and then the instructions afterward. Some parts of it are very hard. The punishment part, for instance."

"Punishment?" said Nickie.

Mrs. Beeson turned a corner and headed up Fern Street, walking so quickly that Nickie kept getting left behind. "Yes, for people who just won't cooperate," Mrs. Beeson said. "We can't allow that, can we? It would be letting down everyone else in Yonwood."

"What's the punishment?" Nickie asked.

But Mrs. Beeson must not have heard her over the splash of the rain. "It's such a responsibility," she went on. "I've agonized over it, I must admit. Some of the things she says—I don't know. I hate to think she really means—" She shook her head, staring down at the wet sidewalk. "I just hesitate to—"

Then suddenly she stopped, and a little rush of water flowed off the top of her pink hat onto Nickie's head. Her voice became strong again. "What am I saying? I hesitate? Just because something is hard? Just because it means making a sacrifice? No, no, no. That's what faith is, isn't it? Believing even when you don't understand."

Nickie looked up at her. She was gazing at the sky, her eyes shining, paying no attention to the rain falling on her face. "It is?" Nickie said.

"Yes," said Mrs. Beeson. "It is." And with that, she hurried away.

Back at Greenhaven, Nickie went upstairs, passing some men who were polishing the floors with a roaring machine. Mrs. Beeson, she thought, seemed more fired up than ever, like an engine revved to a higher level. Nickie had the feeling something was going to happen.

In the nursery, Otis greeted her energetically. "Oty-Oty-Otis!" she cried. She rolled him over and scratched his pink tummy, and he paddled his feet and stretched his head out so she could scratch his throat, too. "You are a darling, Otis," she said. She lifted him up onto the window seat, and she turned on the lamp. As the rain pounded down outside, she started in again on the stack of papers she'd taken from the big trunk.

She found some letters written to "Mommy and Daddy" from a girl at summer camp in 1955, and an article cut from a newspaper's social pages about an elegant birthday party held at Greenhaven in 1940. After setting aside still more bent postcards and ancient Christmas cards and faded photographs, she came upon a fragile old envelope with a strange-looking letter inside that she thought at first was just a page of crazy scribbling. But when she looked at it closely, she could see that it was writing after all. It was a sort of *double* writing. The letter writer (someone named Elizabeth) had written on the page in the usual way and then had turned the paper and written right *across* what she'd written before! The result looked totally unreadable—like two barbed-wire fences laid on top of each other. But she found that if she held the paper in a certain way, slightly tipped, the writing going one direction faded into the background, and the writing going the other direction became clear.

The letter was dated January 4, 1919. Most of it wasn't really worth the trouble it took to read. Elizabeth wrote about ordinary things: visitors who'd arrived, a party, new clothes, a new horse. One bit was intriguing, though: "I hope your dear mother is not so terribly sad as she was. I see as I write this that it's been a year today since the fever took darling baby Frederick. Such a great sorrow! But time must have healed her a little by now."

Nickie imagined the mother, young and beautiful and wearing one of those long, slender dresses she'd

January 4, 1919

My dearest Amelia,

Samuel arrived this afternoon
with his new wife Sarah. She is such a
darling! She was wearing a brown
traveling dress, but later she changed
into a beautiful mauve wool from
Paris. I long to wear Paris fashions!
There is to be a large dinner party on
Saturday. All the Porter cousins are
coming, and I'll wear my green silk
with the lace trim.

Have I told you about Father's
new horse? He's a very fine one, coal
black with a white star. Father let me
name him! I chose the name Galahad. I
long to ride him, but Father won't

seen in the photographs, sitting in anguish at the bed-side of her baby, not able to give him the right medi-cine because it hadn't been invented yet. It would be dreadful to watch your baby die. No wonder she was still sad a year later.

She decided to keep this letter because of the strange way it was written. She set it on the shelf with the picture of the twins.

It was time to meet Crystal for dinner. Nickie walked toward downtown. Overhead, she heard the fighter jets again, roaring across the sky, above the clouds. She shivered, thinking of the president's deadline. Only three days left.

The whole town had a gloomy, closed-in look tonight. Nearly all the houses were dark, their blinds and curtains drawn. A small house on Birch Street had lighted windows, though, and as Nickie passed she saw a police car draw up in front of it. Good, she thought. They're going to make those people follow the rules.

When she got to the Cozy Corner and pushed open the door, warm food-scented air greeted her. The restaurant was dim because its lights were off, but candles on each table made it seem cozy anyhow. She spotted Crystal right away: she was sitting with her back to Nickie, at a table beside the window, and across from her sat a tall man with a little mustache. It must be Len, the real estate agent. Why was *he* here? Crystal hadn't said she was meeting Len for dinner. She'd said she and *Nickie* would have dinner together and Nickie would tell about her adventures. Not that she had any adventures she wanted to tell about.

Len saw her standing there. He said something to Crystal, and she turned around and called, "Nickie! Here we are!"

When Nickie sat down, Crystal said, "I talked to your mother today. She got a card from your father. Didn't say where he was or what he was doing, but he said he might have a surprise for her pretty soon."

"He must be coming home!" Nickie said. "Oh, I hope he is." She missed her father with a terrible ache all of a sudden. He called her his chickadee and made paper airplanes for her. She wished he were here right now.

She wanted to ask if her mother had said anything else, but Crystal had moved on to another subject. "We've been planning," she said. "We're thinking this Saturday for the open house."

"Crossing our fingers for good weather," said Len, grinning, and holding up two sets of crossed fingers and wagging them at Nickie.

"That means a lot of work has to get done during the next three days," said Crystal. She sounded quite cheerful about it. She took her notebook out of her purse, and she and Len started in on still another to-do list as if it were the most fun thing in the world.

Nickie ordered her soup and stared out the window. The last of the sunlight edged the top of the mountain in gold. Someone in a "Don't Do It!" T-shirt walked by, and someone else with a cell phone clapped to her ear. Across the street, a black car pulled into the gas station. Hoyt McCoy got out of it. Just the sight of him made Nickie feel guilty. She watched as he filled up his gas tank, and she was glad when he drove off, heading down the road that led to the highway.

Dinner took forever. Crystal's to-do list got longer and longer, and every item had to be discussed in tedious detail. Now and then Nickie commented on something, but no one paid attention to her. She was just about to say she was going back to Greenhaven when there was a loud tap on the window next to her. Startled, she turned. Outside stood Grover, his eyes round and worried-looking.

"Who's *that*?" said Crystal.

"The handyman's son," Nickie said. "I sort of know him." She laughed, thinking he was joking around as usual. But instead of breaking into a smile or a maniac face, Grover shook his head and beckoned to her. His mouth moved, making exaggerated words: "Come out." Nickie's smile froze on her face. What was wrong?

She stood up from the table. "I have to go ask him something," she said, and before Crystal and Len could say a word, she dashed out the door and hurried after Grover.

CHAPTER 20

Orders

He was waiting for her a few steps farther up the block, outside a shoe store.

"What's the matter?" she said. "Why were you looking at me like that?"

"Something bad has happened," he said. "You know my snakes?"

She nodded.

"They told me I have to get rid of them."

"What? Who told you?"

"Brenda Beeson. I went home for lunch and there was a note for me in the mailbox. It said snakes are touched with evil and it isn't good to keep them and I have to get rid of them."

"Oh," said Nickie, with a shock of dismay.

"Someone must have told her," Grover said. "I think I know who: my so-called friend Martin."

Nickie didn't answer. She stared at a man taking

the display tables of on-sale shoes inside for the night. She didn't want to meet Grover's eyes.

"He was lurking around outside my shed a few days ago," Grover went on. "Someone was, anyway. He ran away before I could see who it was." He scowled. "I don't *want* to get rid of my snakes."

Nickie felt a sickening dizziness. She couldn't remember, all of a sudden, whose side she was on. Was she God's helper or Grover's friend? Her mind went numb. She didn't know what to say.

"I had to tell someone," Grover said. "I saw you in there, so . . ." He shrugged, looking at her curiously, probably wondering why she was standing there like a dummy.

Without her even wanting it to, the truth pushed its way out of her. "It wasn't a he," she said, looking down at the sidewalk.

"What? Who wasn't?"

"It was me. Outside your shed. It was me who told her about the snakes."

Grover's mouth dropped open. "You? *You?*"

"I've been helping her," Nickie said. "Looking for things that are bad, you know, helping her root them out. I didn't *know* if keeping snakes was bad. I just asked her about it. That's all I did."

"Why are you *helping* her?" Grover said. He flung his hands out and looked at her with an "I can't believe this" expression.

"Because I want to fight against evil," Nickie said. "Find trouble spots. Help keep everything on the side of good, so we'll be safe."

"You know what they're going to do if I don't get rid of my snakes?" Grover said.

"What?"

"Put one of those bracelet things on me. Hah!" he cried out suddenly. A woman passing by gave him a startled look. "Let 'em try it. They're never gonna touch me."

"What bracelet things?" Nickie asked.

"You don't know about them?" Grover circled his wrist with his thumb and forefinger. "They hum. They go *MMMMmmmm-MMMMmmmm*. Some little non-stop battery thing powers them. You can't get them off, even with a hammer or a hacksaw, because they're made of something incredibly hard. Anybody they say is a sinner gets one. Nobody can talk to a person with a bracelet, and they won't take it off till you either quit sinning or leave."

"Leave?"

"Leave town. Move somewhere else."

"That must be what I've heard, then," Nickie said. "Twice I heard it."

"There's three or four people who have them right now. They don't come out much. They don't want to be seen. Jonathan Small has one. So does Ricky Platt."

"What did they do wrong?"

"I don't know about Ricky, but Jonathan sings," said Grover. "No one is supposed to, since the Prophet said 'No singing.' But he sings these loud show tunes in the shower every morning. His neighbors heard him, and the cops came and snapped the bracelet on him. He said he wouldn't quit singing, but I think he's about ready to change his mind. That bracelet thing drives a person crazy." He twisted his lips in a disgusted way. "A whole lot of people got these letters in their mailboxes. I heard about two of 'em already: The Elwoods got one for yelling at each other. Maryessa Brown got one for smoking. And you should have seen what happened to old Hoyt McCoy. They brought out the whole police force and tried to arrest him. I saw it—I was there."

Nickie's heart had started beating rapidly. "Maybe you should let the snakes go," she said.

"Why should I?" he said. "What harm are they doing?"

"They could bite someone," Nickie said weakly.

"There's a lock on the shed! No one goes in there but me!" Grover was shouting now, and people passing by were frowning at him. His face took on its wild-eyed look. "And anyway," he yelled, "they're *not venomous snakes!*"

Nickie stepped back. "I'm sorry," she said. "I was just trying to . . . I don't know, to do the right thing."

She took a deep, shaky breath. "If they try to put one of those bracelets on you, what will you do?"

"Run. They won't catch me." Grover's chin jutted out, and his lips pressed together in a hard line. He pointed a finger at her and shook it in her face. "You should *think* about what's the right thing to do. Not just take someone's word for it." And with that he turned around and stalked away, leaving Nickie standing beside the door of the shoe store, with dark feelings swirling through her like storm clouds.

The storm in her mind got worse when she tried to sleep that night. She couldn't stop thinking about the blue envelopes. Mrs. Beeson must have given one to every person who was doing something they'd decided was wrong. How many of them were people Nickie herself had talked about? And were they all going to do what they were told? Or were there others like Grover, who would refuse? And what *was* the right thing to do?

She didn't feel well. Her stomach was all unsettled. She lay in bed for a long time, not sleeping, thinking about Grover's snakes, and the humming bracelets, and the Prophet, and the president, and God, and about good versus evil, until her mind was a swirl of confusion. Finally, she crept out of bed. She felt her way down the hall in the dark to the back stairs, and she tiptoed up to the third floor and into the nursery.

Otis, who'd been asleep on the bed that had been Amanda's, jumped down and ran to her, wagging his rear end, and Nickie picked him up and got into the bed herself. She could feel the warm spot where he'd been lying—it was right by her knees. She put him back there and laid one arm across his furry body, and after that she felt better. But she didn't sleep soundly that night. A dark feeling stayed with her. She wasn't sure if it was guilt or dread.

CHAPTER 21

Getting Ready for the Open House

For the next two days, Wednesday and Thursday, Nickie worked with Crystal at Greenhaven, helping her get ready for the open house. Crystal gave her the assignment of cleaning and neatening the rooms on the third floor. "We won't bother to make those rooms beautiful," she said, "but they can at least be presentable. Get rid of mess and cobwebs, sweep up the dead bugs, take extra furniture down to the basement, that sort of thing." She cast her critical gaze around the front parlor, where they were standing. "The rest of the house," she said, "has to be as elegant as possible. I think we can manage it. The house has good bones."

Once each day, Crystal came up to the third floor to see how the work was going, and Nickie had to quickly close Otis into the hall closet and put the radio on loud to disguise any sounds he might make. Luckily, Crystal wasn't very interested in the rooms on the third floor. All she wanted was for them not to look too awful. She glanced in, said Nickie was doing a good job, and went back downstairs.

As she worked, Nickie turned over the problem of goodness in her mind. On Thursday evening, as they were sitting in the kitchen having a dinner of canned soup and soda crackers, and listening to the news on the radio, she asked Crystal her question.

"Crystal," she said. "How do you tell if something is good or bad?"

Crystal was exhausted from rearranging furniture and hauling boxes of stuff down to the local thrift shop. "You mean like a good or bad book?" she said. "A good or bad movie?"

"No," Nickie said, "I mean like something you do. How do you know if it's a good thing to do or not?"

On the radio, the news announcer broke off in the middle of a sentence, and there was a sudden silence. Then he said, "We have a bulletin from the president. One moment."

The president's voice came on, not quite as smooth as usual. Instead of answering Nickie's question, Crystal held up one finger and said, "Listen."

"One day remains," the president said, "before the deadline we have issued to the Phalanx Nations. I regret to say no progress has been made. Our resolve is firm: we will not back down in the face of threats from godless evildoers. Citizens should prepare for possible large-scale conflict. Please refer to the Homeland Security website at www . . ."

Crystal turned down the radio. She frowned and broke a few soda crackers into her soup. "It sounds bad," she said. "We ought to be all right here, but I'm worried about your mother in the city."

"Let's call her, then," said Nickie, "and tell her to come."

"No, I wouldn't want her traveling right now. I'm not really sure what to do." She turned up the radio again, but the president was finished, and the newsman was reporting on a terrorist group that had taken a hundred hostages and was refusing to release them until they swore to follow the one true faith.

"Could you answer my question now?" said Nickie. "About how you tell if something is good or bad?"

"It's a deep question," Crystal said, "and I'm deeply tired. I guess if I had to answer, I'd say that you look to see if what you're doing causes harm. If it hurts anyone. If so, it's probably not good."

"What if it doesn't hurt any *people*," said Nickie, "or even any animals, but it hurts God?"

"Hurts God? How can God be hurt?"

"Well, I mean if what you do goes against what God says."

"You'd have to know what he says, then, wouldn't you? Assuming he's up there saying anything." Crystal swallowed a spoonful of soup. "It's too deep for me," she said. "I just want to eat my dinner and go to bed. And by the way, your mom called again and read me another one of those odd postcards from your dad."

Nickie jumped up. "Did you write it down? Where is it?"

"It's here somewhere." Crystal went out to the hall. "Here." She handed Nickie a scrap of paper.

It said:

Dear Rachel and Nickie,

How is everything with you? Here it's work as usual. I am doing all right, though I miss you both.

Love, Dad

P.S. Nickie, I was thinking about that movie we went to for your ninth birthday. Wasn't it called "Snowblind"?

Nickie thought back to when she turned nine. She remembered it well. She and Kate and Sophy had gone ice-skating. There was no movie. So this confirmed it:

either her father was losing his mind, or he was sending a message in some sort of code. She would crack it. She was sure she could. She took the postcard messages into her bedroom, spread them out on the bed, and began to study them in earnest. And after a while, she had an idea about what the key to the code might be.

On Friday morning, Nickie awoke and instantly knew that she had to find out what had happened to Grover and his snakes. If he was still mad at her, too bad; she couldn't bear not to know.

Crystal said she was meeting Len for breakfast so they could discuss last-minute open-house details. "Want to come?" she said, and of course Nickie said no. As soon as Crystal had left, she ran upstairs to feed Otis and take him outside, and when that was done she headed for Grover's house.

It was very cold. Iron-gray clouds hung like a ceiling over the town. Main Street was strangely quiet. As usual, small clusters of people stood inside the stores with TVs on, but when Nickie glanced in, she didn't see the president on the screen. She couldn't tell what was on—it looked like an old movie of some kind. But she didn't stop to wonder about it. She was in a hurry.

Granny Carrie saw her coming. "You won't find him here," she said as Nickie came up the steps.

"I won't? Where is he?"

"Up in the woods somewheres. They came and clamped one of them bracelets on him this morning early, and he took off."

Nickie stood still where she was, with one foot on the porch and the other on the step. "A bracelet?"

"Yep," said Granny Carrie. She pressed her lips together. "*MMMMMM-mmmm-MMMMM-mmmm*," she said, "Nasty thing."

"He didn't go to school?"

"I doubt it," said Granny Carrie. "With the noise that thing was making, they'd-a probably thrown him out."

"So he didn't let his snakes go, then," said Nickie.

"Said he didn't see why he should."

"How did they catch him? He said he'd run."

"Ambushed him," said Granny Carrie. "Teddy Crane and that old Bill Willard jumped on him from behind the garage when he set out for school. Then he ran off, and the two of them came here and told us what they'd done."

"I'm going to go find him," said Nickie.

"Better not," Granny Carrie said. "His pa's already gone up there after him. No point in you going. You don't know your way around in the woods. He could be anywhere."

"But that terrorist is in the woods," Nickie said.

"So I've heard," said Granny Carrie, frowning and rocking. "It does make a person worry. We've got a lot to worry about today." She waved a hand toward the window, from which came the sound of the TV. "That deadline the president set is up. We're waiting to hear if there's going to be war."

CHAPTER 22

An Indoor Universe

Nickie turned away from Grover's house with her mind whirling. The president's deadline! That's why people were gathered in the stores. They were waiting to hear his announcement. Why was an old movie on, though? Had they started the war without telling anyone? She glanced at the sky, almost expecting to see bombers streaking overhead.

She didn't know what to do. It was true that there was no point in trying to find Grover. Even if she did find him, how could she help? And she certainly couldn't keep a war from happening. Her Goal #3 seemed silly now—how could she possibly do anything to help the messed-up world? She was just a kid.

She walked down the road, hardly noticing where she was going, staring down at the pavement, kicking now and then at a rock. She thought of Grover, a humming bracelet clapped onto his wrist, fleeing up into the mountains, where probably a dangerous person was hiding out. She thought of Hoyt McCoy, accused by police of something he hadn't done. These things were her fault. Somehow she had done wrong by trying to do right.

She trudged on until she came to Raven Road, and there she turned left. She hadn't planned to go this way; her feet just seemed to carry her. When she got to Hoyt McCoy's driveway, her feet stopped. She stared at his "No Trespassing" sign. She gazed up the driveway, past the row of looming trees to the place where the drive curved around toward the house. Part of her wanted to hurry on past. But another part thought she should go in there and tell him she was sorry for what had happened. Was she brave enough? The very thought of it made her stomach shift and her hands get clammy. But she started up the driveway anyhow. She would just knock on his door, apologize very fast, and come away. She was brave enough for that.

The house was as dark and silent this time as it had been before. From a distance, she checked the gable window. It was closed. Nothing that looked like a gun or a telescope stuck out of any of the house's windows. This gave her courage. When she got closer, she realized Hoyt's car wasn't there. Good! Now if she just had a bit of paper and a pencil stub in her pocket, as she usually did—

But behind her she heard the sound of an engine

and the crackle of gravel. She turned, and there was Hoyt McCoy in his black car, coming toward her. He'd seen her, of course; she couldn't leave. So she waited, with her heart thudding.

"Ah," said Hoyt, getting out of the car. "The other trespasser."

Nickie managed to speak. "I—I came to say I'm sorry," she stammered, "about what happened."

"You mean the invasion of the Beeson Police?"

"Yes. Well, it was because . . . I thought you were going to . . . to shoot me."

"I do not shoot people," said Hoyt. He opened the rear door of the car and took out a battered suitcase. "I may not *like* people, but I do not shoot them."

"I just thought," said Nickie, "that you had a gun . . . you know, aiming out your window."

"And my question for *you* is this." Hoyt set down the suitcase, put his hands on his hips, and glared at her. "Why were you here, on my property, looking at my windows in the first place?"

Nickie had no answer for this question. It was no good to say she was trying to do the right thing. Deep down, she'd suspected that looking in windows and snooping around people's houses was probably more wrong than right, no matter what the reason for doing it. So she just stood there, staring down at the ground.

"But of course I *know* why," Hoyt McCoy went on. "Brenda Beeson sent you. Did she send the boy, too?"

"What boy?"

"The boy who sneaked behind my house a week ago. The boy who was lurking about when those cops tried to snatch me. Skinny boy, hair falling in his face."

"Oh, Grover. No, she didn't send him." For a second, the thought of Grover in the woods came to her; she pushed it away. "Well, I have to go now," she said. She'd done what she came to do.

"Wait one moment," said Hoyt McCoy.

Nickie's heart gave a bump.

"I have just returned from a tense encounter which I believe has had the result I hoped for. That puts me in a rather generous mood, rare for me." He walked up his front steps and turned to face her. "I'd like to show you," he said, "that a person may be gruff and somewhat on the sloppy side without being a madman or a criminal. But probably you would decline to step inside my house."

"Well, thank you very much," Nickie said, with her heart beating harder, "but I really have to go."

"I thought so," said Hoyt. "A wise choice, in general, though in this case unnecessarily cautious. Still, you might be willing just to look in from where you are." He took his keys from his pocket, opened the door, stepped in, and stood to the side, so that Nickie could look past him. She saw a wide hall. On either side was an arched opening that led to a room, and down at the end, the hall opened into still another room. Even though it was daytime, the windows were all covered with blinds and curtains; dim electric light bulbs filled the rooms with a yellowish gloom. Signs of careless housekeeping were everywhere: in the hall she saw stacks of books on the floor, clothes hanging from doorknobs, a table strewn with loose change and bits of hardware and scraps of paper. From what she could see of the other rooms, they were just as messy.

But why was he showing her all this? Shouldn't she turn around and run? She took a few steps backward—but somehow, curiosity held her there.

"I am not interested," said Hoyt, "in the dull daily world of chat and tidiness, of keeping up appearances, of being nice and polite and well groomed. No one who doesn't like my looks or my house need ever come near me, and that will suit me well. My world is the heavens, both by day and by night." He raised a hand and turned slightly. "Watch," he said.

Nickie heard the snap of a switch. Instantly, the lights in the house went out, leaving a darkness that would have been complete except for the light from the open front door. Again a bolt of fear shot through her, and she skittered backward a few more steps. Was he going to come out from his strange den and grab her? But a moment later she stood still again, because she saw something happening in the darkness.

The walls and the ceiling had begun to glow. Gradually, they changed from black to a deep midnight blue, as if they were made not of plaster but of glass, like a television screen. Tiny points of light appeared, first just a few here and a few there, and then more and more, until the signs of an untidy daily life receded into shadows, and the rooms of Hoyt McCoy's house became star-spangled chambers of night.

"The effect is better, of course, if the front door isn't standing wide open," said Hoyt. "You may come in and see if you like, but if you're still afraid of me I won't insist."

Nickie just stood there, staring and speechless.

"It took quite a while to customize this house," Hoyt said. "People used to peer over the fence wanting to see how I was remodeling. They were dismayed when the house looked exactly the same after the work was done as before." He laughed—a dry *heh-heh*. "The heavens are my habitat," he said. "Also my job, though as a rule I do not speak of it."

This reminded Nickie of what Grover had said. "Do you crack open the sky?" she asked.

Hoyt raised his eyebrows. "Who told you that?"

"Grover. He said he saw it."

"Ah, yes, so he did." Hoyt smiled dryly. "He's an observant sort. Most people simply write it off as lightning."

"What is it, then?"

"Not something I choose to speak of at this time," said Hoyt. "I have been extraordinarily busy these last few days, involved in some very delicate, high-level conversations. Right now I am satisfied but exhausted. Far too exhausted to explain anything."

"Well," said Nickie, pointing in through the door, "all that is really beautiful." It was. It was as if Hoyt's front door had become a porthole to the universe. She longed to step inside and see it up close, have it surround her, as if she were floating in space. But she still didn't feel quite brave enough. If only Hoyt had been like a kindly old uncle, then she would have. But he was so big and rumpled and shaggy and grouchy—she was still afraid of him, though it did begin to seem that she needn't be.

"Thank you," she said. "I love seeing it. Is it the whole universe?"

"Oh, no," said Hoyt. "Just a small portion of one universe, ours. If I had several billion more houses, I might have room for a few other universes as well."

Other universes. Nickie thought of her great-grandfather's notes. But she could barely get the idea of one universe into her mind, to say nothing of others. "I'd like to see it," she said. "But . . . maybe I'll come some other time."

"Simply ring the bell," said Hoyt. "Trespassers are not welcome. Certain selected visitors are. You may include yourself among them." With a brief nod—no smile—he closed the door, and the universe disappeared.

Back at Greenhaven, Nickie wandered through the house, too stirred up to settle to anything. She gazed at the ancestors in their gold frames; she ran her fingers along the curves of the banister; she stared at her reflection in the great dining room mirror. Up in the nursery, she rocked in the rocking chair beneath the glow of the lamp, holding Otis on her lap and running her hand from his head to his tail, over and over.

Around four-thirty, when Crystal still wasn't back from wherever she was, she took Otis down for his afternoon outing. To her surprise, there were people on the street, walking as if they had an appointment somewhere.

Quickly, she took Otis back upstairs and came down again. As she went out the front door, she saw Martin among the people passing. She ran up to him. "What's happening?"

"You didn't hear?" Martin looked down his nose at Nickie. "There's a meeting. Mrs. Beeson called it. She wants to speak to everyone. It's urgent. You should come—it's at the church."

"Do you know what it's about?" Nickie asked.

"No," said Martin. "But it must be important." He set off down the sidewalk again. "You should come," he said again, over his shoulder. "And your aunt, too."

Crystal wouldn't be interested; Nickie was sure of

that. But she herself would go, of course. She had to know what the meeting was about. She dashed back into the house to get her jacket—the sun was down now, and the temperature was dropping—and then she joined the flow of people moving toward the church.

CHAPTER 23

The Emergency Meeting

From the uphill and downhill neighborhoods, people converged on Main Street—frowning, worried-looking men, mothers holding the hands of young children, older children following along, unusually quiet. Everyone was unusually quiet, in fact; when they spoke at all, it was in low voices, just to exchange a few questions: What's this about, do you know? Have no idea. Must be something serious. Maybe something new from the Prophet. Maybe so. They hurried past the dark windows of the stores, which had closed early, down past the deserted park, down toward the very end of Main Street—a stream of people, almost all the citizens of Yonwood. Though not quite all, Nickie remembered. Hoyt McCoy wouldn't be here, and Grover wouldn't, because he was up in the woods somewhere, and no doubt there were a few other

Yonwood citizens who didn't come when Brenda Beeson called.

But certainly most of the town was now pouring into the narrow, upright building that was the Church of the Fiery Vision. Once Nickie got past the crush of people at the door, she saw a long room filled with rows of wooden pews. High in the walls were windows of stained glass, but because the sky outside was growing dark, she couldn't make out the pictures in them. The light inside the church was dim, too. It came from candles placed in dozens of spots around the room. They lit up the aisles and the seats, but the space above, up to the ceiling, was a gulf of darkness.

Quickly and quietly, people filed into the pews and sat down. Nickie sat toward the back. Then came long moments when nothing happened. People whispered and rustled, waiting. At last a door opened behind the pulpit, and Mrs. Beeson came out. She climbed up the steps to the pulpit and stood there looking out at the crowd. The whispering immediately died down.

There was no hat of any kind today. Mrs. Beeson's hair was fluffed out in a cloud around her head, and she wore a red dress with her round blue Tower button pinned to the front. She stood looking out at them in silence for a long time, her eyes flitting from one face to another. At last she spoke. There was a wave of creaks and rustles as everyone leaned forward to hear.

"Well, friends," she said, "we're in a dark time."

There was a murmur of agreement from the crowd.

"Our Prophet has seen a dreadful disaster in the world's future. It could be the war that might be coming. It could have to do with the terrorist in our woods."

The crowd murmured again.

"But she's also tried to tell us how to be safe from this disaster. I call that a miracle. It's like being taken under God's wing."

Mrs. Beeson smiled, and Nickie could tell that the people in the room were feeling that smile's warm glow.

"And so most of us," Mrs. Beeson went on, "have done our best to do what our Prophet tells us to do. It's not always easy to know what that is. Sometimes the Prophet says things that even I can't interpret. She says 'No words,' for example. Unless she means swear-words, which we don't say anyhow, I must admit I'm mystified. And there's something else she says that until now I've thought I must be hearing wrongly. But as danger comes closer, I'm forced to believe she means exactly what she says."

Mrs. Beeson paused. She stood still, her blue eyes scanning the crowd. She looked like a queen, Nickie thought, in her ruby red dress, with the light from the candles gilding her hair. The people in the church seemed to hold their breath.

Finally, Mrs. Beeson squared her shoulders and

spoke. "What I am about to say is for the good of us all," she said. "We must be obedient, whether we understand or not. God's ways are beyond our knowing." She paused again, for a long time. Tension twisted in Nickie's stomach. People sat so still that the whole room was utterly silent.

When Mrs. Beeson spoke next, her voice was hardly above a whisper, but it was so fierce that you could hear every word. "Althea has said it over and over, but I haven't wanted to hear it. 'No dogs,' she says. 'No dogs.' It's quite clear. Somehow, our dogs are standing in the way."

"What?!" cried a woman a few rows up, but someone else shushed her.

Mrs. Beeson's voice rose. "Yes," she said. "I see it now. I see it in myself, in my own feelings for my little Sausage." She leaned forward, gripping the pulpit with both hands. "Why should we give an animal love that should go to our families? Why should we give an animal love that should go to God? We have to act, my dear friends. I know it's hard, but the dogs—all of them—must go."

Nickie's heart started rapid-fire beating. Dogs must go? What was she saying?

A clamor arose from the people in the church. Voices cried, What? and No! but Mrs. Beeson spread her arms out and stood like an angel about to rise. "Listen!" she cried.

Everyone grew silent again.

"It's painful, I know," she said. "But terrible times demand extraordinary sacrifices. Seems to me what the Prophet is saying to us is this: the more we say no to the things of the world, all those things we're too attached to, the more we can say yes to God. It's what I've told you before: when you have faith that you're right—you *know* it from the bottom of your soul— you're willing to do anything for it. Anything."

At that, the people grew silent again. A few stood up and left the church—one man shouted "She's wrong!" as he went out the door—but all the rest stayed. Nickie saw some of them look at each other with stern, brave looks and nod. Then they looked back at her again, waiting for instructions.

"It will be like this," she said. "The day after tomorrow, I will send a bus to all dog-owning households. You will put your dog aboard the bus, and the driver will take the dogs to a wild place many miles from here, where the dogs will be free to go back into nature, where they belong. No animal will be harmed, and we here in Yonwood will have followed our instructions to the letter. We will be free to love God with all our hearts."

Nickie felt as if she'd been set on fire. They won't take Otis, she thought. Never.

But she realized after a moment that she didn't have to worry about Otis. No one knew that Greenhaven was "a dog-owning household." The only people besides herself who knew about Otis were Amanda and Grover, and they wouldn't hurt him. She would keep him safe—she'd be extra super careful when she took him out to pee—and when the house was sold, she'd take him away with her, back to the city.

Because she knew now that she would fail at her Goal #1, which was to live at Greenhaven with her parents. She still loved Greenhaven, and Yonwood, too, but she no longer wanted to live in a place where Mrs. Beeson and her Prophet delivered instructions from God.

CHAPTER 24

The Bracelet

On Friday morning, as Grover was on his way to school, two men had jumped him as he passed the car-repair garage. They'd been standing behind a gate that led into an alley beside the building, and when Grover came past they simply stepped out into his path and blocked his way. Before he realized what was happening, each of them grabbed one of his arms. One of them whipped the bracelet out of his pocket, snapped it around Grover's right wrist, clicked a button on a remote control, and the bracelet was activated. It started up its noise: *MMMM-mmmm-MMMMM-mmmmm.*

He wrenched free and ran, but by then, of course, it was too late. The noise screamed from his wrist. He shook his arm as if the thing were a scorpion biting him, as if it were a cloud of bees attacking, but there was no stopping it. Get away, get away, was all he could think. He ran around the far side of his house and down Woodfield Road, where there were fewer people, though the few he passed stared at him in horror. He didn't look at them. Get away, get away. He ran past the school, staying far out at the edge of the playing fields, past the end of Main Street, where the windows of the Cozy Corner Café were still dark, and then, all the time with the noise streaming out behind him like a kite tail, he ran up the path into the woods.

When he'd run uphill for ten minutes or so, he stopped. The whine of the bracelet—*MMMM-mmmm-MMMMM-mmmmm*—zinged around his head like a monster mosquito. He had to do something about it. Though the morning was cold, he was warm from running. So he took off his jacket and the sweatshirt he was wearing underneath it. He put his jacket back on, and he wrapped the sweatshirt around his wrist, tying it as tightly as he could by the sleeves. It made his arm into a sort of club, with a great lump at the end. The sound was deadened, but not silenced. He could still hear it, and of course anyone walking in the woods— human or animal—would be able to hear it, too. So he unwound the sweatshirt. He took off his jacket and his T-shirt, put his jacket back on (because he wouldn't be able to once he'd made his hand into a club), and wrapped the T-shirt around the bracelet as a first layer. Then he wrapped the sweatshirt around that. This made a wad as big as a soccer ball. His arm looked like a giant lollipop. It might make a good weapon, he thought. Too bad Teddy Crane and Bill Willard weren't around for him to clobber.

The double wrapping muted the noise of the bracelet down to a faint hum. It was good enough. Grover strode on.

What he was going to do he didn't know. He had no plan, other than to escape the town and all the pitying, tut-tutting faces that would be trained on him— people on the street, his teachers, the other kids at school. No. He would figure out a way to get the thing off. He wouldn't go home until he had.

He climbed fast, fueled by rage. After half an hour or so, he came to the place he'd been a few days before, where the path led down to the stream. This was a good spot to stop for a moment, he thought. He was thirsty. He'd have a drink.

As he knelt by the stream and splashed water into his mouth with his left hand, he remembered the person he'd seen moving through the woods when he was last here—the pale patch off in the distance. For a second, with water dripping down his chin, he stopped moving and listened for footsteps. But as soon as he wasn't making the noise of footsteps himself, crunching over twigs, rustling in the leaves, all he could hear was the thin whine of the bracelet, sounding through its wrappings: *MMMM-mmmm-MMMMM-mmmmm,* like a faraway siren.

So he wiped his wet hand on his pants and walked on. He thought of singing really loud to cover up the noise. But if there *was* some evil person lurking up here, singing would just attract his attention. He tried to tune his ears to the tweeting of the birds instead.

The path wound up the mountainside. Every now and then he came to a place where the trees thinned out and he had a view over the town below. School would have started by now. They'd notice he wasn't there. Would Bill and Teddy have gone to his house after they'd clapped the bracelet on him and told his parents? Would anyone come looking for him?

By midday, he was close to the top of the ridge, and he was starting to feel hungry. He happened to have a couple of stale crackers in his jacket pocket, so he ate those. But it wasn't much of a lunch. At this season of the year, he wouldn't be able to find much in the woods that he could eat. The berries would be gone, and although there were lots of mushrooms, he didn't know enough about them to tell the edible ones from the poisonous. He'd just have to be hungry for a while, that's all. Good thing he'd had a big breakfast.

When he came to a small open field, he decided to stop for a while and attack the bracelet. There was a shelf of rock at the edge of the field, large and low. Here he sat down. He unwrapped the sweatshirt from around his wrist, and then the T-shirt. The hideous noise wailed out into the air. Grover winced. It was like having skewers poked in his ears.

The bracelet was a flat metal band about a quarter of an inch thick, a dull silver color. There was a small hinge at one point on it, and a couple of grooves that went all the way around. The sound came from inside, but Grover couldn't see any way of getting at it—no switch or slot or sliding panel.

Maybe he could just slip the thing off. He curled his hand into a tube shape and tried to work the bracelet over his knuckles—but it wouldn't go. He slipped the fingers of his left hand under it and pulled as hard as he could, hoping to break the hinge, but all he accomplished was to make the edge of the bracelet dig into his skin. In furious frustration, he banged the bracelet against the rock, but the silver surface of it was barely even scratched. The noise went on without a pause, *MMMM-mmmm-MMMMM-mmmmm*, making him want to scream.

One more try. He found a rock about the size of a baseball and, placing his wrist on the bigger rock, smashed at the bracelet over and over. After five minutes of pounding, he'd made a tiny dent in the bracelet's surface and a sizable scrape on his hand. With a yell, he flung the rock away and gave up. He put the wrappings back on his wrist. Failure.

He lay back on the warm rock and stared at the

sky, where a hawk was circling far, far above. What had he done wrong? Nothing. Who was he hurting? No one. So why was he being tortured? He didn't know. Had Althea Tower muttered something about snakes? Was there a law against snakes in some holy book? He didn't know. And he didn't know what he could do about any of it.

Stymied, he closed his eyes. The sun shone on him, and he grew sleepy and dozed off.

When he woke up, he could see that it was late afternoon. The shadows of the trees crept across the field, and the air had grown chillier. Grover felt bleak. What was he going to do when night came? What would he do tomorrow? He was hungry, and he was cold, too, because with his T-shirt and his sweatshirt wrapping up his wrist, all he had on was a flannel shirt and his jacket. Which was better, to be warm and have that noise screaming at him, or be cold and without the noise? He decided to be cold, at least for the moment.

For the first time, he realized that he was going to spend the night up here. He hadn't really thought about it before, when all he wanted was to get away. But he saw that he would have to. Darkness would fall before he could get down the trail—and he didn't want to be back in town anyway.

So he'd better use the daylight that was left to get ready. He'd make himself some sort of den to sleep in, and he'd look as hard as he could for some nuts or shriveled-up berries to eat.

First the den. He wanted to be in among the trees, not out in the open. So he crossed to the west side of the field and made his way into the thicket of undergrowth, stamping down brush and breaking off twigs that got in his way. It was like burrowing through barbed wire, he thought, so many stickers and scratchers. Underfoot, the ground was leaf-littered and rocky and uneven. And damp. It wasn't a great place for a campout.

But after creeping around for a while, he found a sort of scooped-out place in the ground surrounded by a group of pines. The pine needles were thick on the ground, and he mounded them up to make a mattress. This wouldn't be too bad, he thought. Now for food.

A few rays of sunlight still fell across the top of the mountain and lit up the trees on the other side of the field. Grover started to make his way out of the woods, back through the brush the way he'd come. But just as he got to the edge of the clearing, he saw, within the trees on the opposite side, something white moving.

He stood still. The trees would hide him, he thought, if he didn't move. If only he had binoculars! His heart began a quick, steady thudding. Could the terrorist hear the faint hum of the bracelet?

The white patch moved slowly. It seemed to be coming toward the clearing. Grover held his breath. He squinted, trying to see more clearly in the failing light. The white patch moved, stood still, moved again, and at last came out from the shelter of the trees and into the field.

And Grover's heart gave a great lurch. This terrorist was not human. And it was not a terrorist, either. It was a bear. A white bear—something Grover had never seen nor heard of.

The bear came out into the field. It walked with a lopsided motion, as if maybe one of its feet hurt. Its nose was down; its head swung slightly from side to side. Its coat, Grover could see, was not pure white at all. It was a dirty cream color, smudged with gray.

It came closer. Grover held his breath. He didn't really think the bear would attack him. He'd caught sight of bears up here before, and he knew that the main thing was not to take the bear by surprise. Make a noise, let it know you were there, and it would turn around and shuffle off. Still, he was nervous. It was almost night, he was all alone, and he was making a strange noise the bear would soon start to hear.

And as soon as he had that thought, the bear lifted its head. It stopped moving and looked straight toward Grover. The last rays of the sun shone on its small round ears, turning them pink.

So Grover did what he knew he should do. He stepped out from the trees and stood in the open. He raised his right arm, so that the humming ball at the end of it stood up in the air like a stop sign. In as strong a voice as he could muster, he called out: "Bear! Here I am! I'm your friend, not your dinner!"

They stared at each other. Grover saw that the bear's nose was a pale tan, and its eyes shone in the slanting sunlight like little rubies. He called out again, waving his arm. "I see what you are!" he said. "You should get away from here! You're not safe!"

And as if it understood, the bear turned away. It didn't hurry. It turned around and trundled back the way it had come. In a few minutes, it had gone into the woods and disappeared.

Grover slept that night on his cushion of pine needles. He covered himself with more pine needles, and he used the wad around his wrist as a pillow. The bracelet whined in his ear and, when he finally fell asleep, made its way into his dreams as a screaming jet plane diving toward him and swooping away, over and over. When he awoke in the morning, he was very cold and very hungry, and he knew there was nothing to do but go home. At least it was Saturday; no one would try to make him go to school.

CHAPTER 25

The Open House

The house looked beautiful on Saturday morning. Its floors were polished, its paint was bright, and the pieces of furniture that remained were the finest antiques of the lot, and dust-free. Big vases stood here and there, with artistically arranged pine branches and bare twigs arching out of them.

Now Crystal was scuttling among the downstairs rooms, looking for anything that might discourage a buyer. Was there a crack in the plaster? Cover it with an antique portrait in a gold frame! A scuffed place on the floor? Put a Persian rug there! She puttered and fussed, fixed and fidgeted, talking the whole time. "The Tiffany lamp! Here would be the perfect spot. And wait, these cushions . . . Nickie, would you get those green ones from the middle bedroom? That's better. Really, it's looking good. Except for . . . hold on a sec . . . maybe the leather-topped game table over here ... Help me move it, Nickie."

Over an hour went by, during which Nickie could not stop thinking about Otis two floors above, needing his breakfast, needing to go outside, ready any second to start whining or barking. But Crystal, for once, wasn't in a hurry.

At ten o'clock, she turned on the radio. "There ought to be some news," she said. She stopped dashing around and sat down to listen. Nickie listened, too. "We are expecting an announcement from the White House at any moment," said the newscaster. "The president's deadline ran out yesterday, but so far there has been no word on the status of the situation."

They kept listening, but no announcement came. There was a report about an earthquake somewhere, and a riot somewhere else, and then something about two movie stars getting married, and finally the announcer came back on and said that there was still no news about the tense international situation and that people should stay tuned.

"It's odd," said Crystal, flicking off the radio. "But at least it's not war. Not yet."

She went back to work. For another half hour, she wandered around adding final touches here and there. Finally she flopped down on the red plush sofa in the front parlor and surveyed what she had done. "Not bad," she said. She checked her watch. "Ten forty-two. We open at eleven. Len should be here any minute."

"Do you need me anymore?" Nickie asked.

"No, no," said Crystal, waving a hand. "You go off and play."

"Okay," Nickie said. "I just have to get some stuff from upstairs first."

Crystal nodded. She reached for a spray bottle and squirted a fine mist at a potted fern.

Nickie dashed up the stairs. Poor Otis, poor Otis; if he'd made a puddle on the floor, she wouldn't say a single scolding word. She burst through the door at the top of the stairs, closed it behind her, flung open the nursery door, and there was Otis scrambling backward, yelping and squealing with a desperate tone in his voice. He'd been standing right there, she could picture it, nose to the place where the door would open, waiting for her. She scanned the room. Only one small puddle, which she quickly mopped up.

"Okay, Otis," she said, "just a couple more minutes. I'll be really quick." Otis jumped up and down beside her leg. "I know you're hungry, but we have to get out of here first. You have to be *incredibly quiet.*"

She hooked Otis's leash to his collar and wound it once around his muzzle so he couldn't bark. Then she picked him up and carried him down the hall and down the stairs. She paused at the second floor, listening for Crystal. Heard nothing. Went down the next flight to the door that led to the hall behind the kitchen. Listened again. This time she heard voices.

"Looks great!" said Len's voice. "You do, too."

"Well, thanks! You're such a sweetie."

That was Crystal. They were by the front door, Nickie thought. Good. She darted into the kitchen, grabbed an apple and a muffin from a bowl on the table, opened the door to the back garden, and shouted, "Bye, I'm leaving! Good luck!" Before anyone even answered, she shut the door behind her and took off.

It was not a beautiful day for a walk. Gray clouds hung low and dark in the sky, and the air was cold enough to bite. Nickie had on her warmest jacket and a thick knitted scarf around her neck and a knitted hat that came down over her ears, and she was still chilly. She'd warm up as she walked, probably, but it would be nice if the wind would die down. She snuggled Otis's head up under her chin.

At the end of the block, she went around the corner, turned onto Fern Street, and started up the path that led in among the trees. A few yards along, she stopped and set Otis down on the ground. Instantly, he pulled the leash tight, making a beeline for the base of a tree, where he lifted his back leg and sent a stream of pee against the bark. "Good boy," said Nickie. Suddenly she felt happy and free. The cold didn't matter. The woods stretched before her, mysterious, unexplored. No danger of running into the dog-napping Prophet out here, or any of her spies. And if there was a terror-ist wandering around in the woods—well, if she saw him, she'd just hide, that's all.

So they hiked, Nickie striding along on legs that felt strong and glad to be exercised, and Otis zigzag-ging across the path from one fascinating smell to the next. The ground crackled underfoot—icy dead leaves, brittle twigs, dirt hardened by cold. In all direc-tions stood the endless ranks of gray-brown tree trunks, their bare branches making a dense weave that reminded her of the crosshatched writing on the old letter. Wind rattled the branches against each other, and here and there a few last rags of leaf fell down.

It was a little after eleven o'clock. In a while, she'd find a place to sit, and she'd eat the muffin and the apple she had with her. But now all she wanted to do was walk, and walk fast.

The trail wound back and forth, always sloping upward, but never very steep. Most of the time, all Nickie could see was the deep forest on both sides, but after a while she came to a clearing where the trees thinned out on the downhill side, and she could look down the mountain and see the roofs of the town below. It looked small and peaceful from here. No peo-ple were visible. She tried to make out which house was Greenhaven, but she couldn't tell. It made her a lit-tle sad, this view of Yonwood, the place where she had been sure she wanted to live. In her imagination, it had been so perfect—peaceful and beautiful, safe from the troubles of the cities. If someone had told her then that Yonwood was working to battle the forces of evil by building a shield of goodness, she would have been happy to hear it. Those things were exactly what she wanted. How strange that it could all turn out so differently.

She walked on. It wasn't a steady walk, because Otis had to stop every few yards and thrust his nose beneath a bush or into the leaf litter that covered the ground. Some spots were so interesting that he had to snuffle in them for quite a while. During these times, Nickie stood still and gazed around her. Birds flitted among the branches, twittering in a muted way. Overhead, clouds moved slowly across the sky, so the forest was sometimes in shadow, sometimes in sunlight. When the sun shone down, crystals of frost and patches of ice glistened like glass.

When she'd walked for an hour or so, she started thinking it was time to rest, and time to eat. She looked for somewhere to sit down. A few yards farther on she came to a fallen tree that lay alongside the trail, covered in a tangle of brown stickery vines and furred with green moss along the top. She tore the vines away to make a clear space, and she tied her end of Otis's leash to the stump of a branch sticking up from the log. Then she sat down, took the muffin and the apple out of her paper bag, and ate them both, except for the last chunk of muffin, which she gave to Otis. She crushed the paper bag into a ball and stuck it in her pocket.

That was when she heard the footsteps. There was no mistaking them—firm and steady, a tramp, tramp, tramp that came from above her on the trail, not far distant. Nickie's heart started racing. Could she duck behind a tree? Crouch down behind this fallen log? But Otis had heard the footsteps, too, and after a moment of cocking his head and pricking up his ears, he let out a string of loud barks. So there was no use hiding. Whoever was coming would have heard them already. He would come around the bend in a moment and see them, and Nickie would just have to hope that if it was a terrorist or some other sort of wild person, he would have more important things on his mind than a girl eating lunch.

So she sat frozen on the log and waited, and in a few seconds the person came around the bend, and it wasn't a terrorist; it was Grover.

"Hey!" he cried when he saw her. He stopped and stared. Then he made a face of extreme horror, pulling down the corners of his mouth and making his eyes bulge out. "Aaaaaiiieee!" he yelled. "It's a terrifying terrorist! And a savage monster! Save me, save me!"

"Stop that," said Nickie. Relief swept through her, and she grinned.

Otis bounded over to Grover and stood up against his legs, and Grover stooped to pet him—with his left hand, because his right hand was bundled up in a clump of clothes. When he came closer, Nickie could hear the hum of the bracelet: *MMMM-mmmm-MMMMM-mmmmm.*

"Can I see it?" she said.

"Five dollars per view," said Grover.

"Come on."

So he unwrapped his wrist, and the noise came out loud and shrill in the cold air. Nickie peered at the thing. "It's awful," she said. "You can't break it with a rock or anything?"

"Not without breaking my arm, too. I tried." He wrapped it up again. "What are you doing here?"

"It's the open house today," Nickie said. "I have to keep Otis away. Not just because of the open house, but the Prophet, too."

Grover sat down on the log. "Why?"

Nickie told him what Mrs. Beeson had said. "It's tomorrow. She's going to take all the dogs away."

Grover responded to this by rearing backward and nearly falling off the log, as if knocked off balance by astonishment. "I am stunned," he said.

"Me too," said Nickie. "You don't think she could be right, do you? That dogs take up too much love? Which should go to God?"

"I don't think so," said Grover, sitting up straight again. Otis sniffed at his wrist, which hummed faintly. "I really don't think so."

"But Otis is all right because nobody knows about him. Hardly anybody. You do, but you wouldn't tell, would you?"

"Nope," said Grover. He rumpled Otis's ears. "Guess what?" he said.

"What?"

"I saw the terrorist."

"Not *really*," said Nickie. "Did you?"

"I did." He told her about the bear. "It was an albino," he said. "I'm pretty sure it was, because I've never heard of a white bear. Except polar bears, and there aren't any in North Carolina." He looked thoughtful, and a little sad. "I told it to go away," he said, "for its own good. People here don't like things that are different."

"Was it beautiful?" Nickie said.

"Not really. It was sort of dirty-looking. It had smudges on it. And it was limping."

"Were you afraid?" Nickie asked.

But Grover didn't answer. He was staring into space with his eyebrows raised. "I just thought of something," he said.

"What?"

"The broken window. I bet it was the bear. Put its foot through the glass."

"You mean at the restaurant?"

"Right. Snatched up that chicken and snagged the napkin with a claw, I bet. And that blood. She said it was an *R*, but I always thought it was just a blot. It was bear blood. Bet you anything."

He explained, and Nickie listened. "Bear blood," she said wonderingly. "No one guessed."

They sat without talking for a few moments. The bracelet hummed beneath its wrappings.

"You have to get that thing off you," said Nickie. "What are you going to do?"

Grover stood up. The wind was blowing harder now, and dark clouds were coming in from the east. "It doesn't matter about my snakes, I guess. I can let them go. I studied them a lot already. And in the summer, when I leave, I was going to let them go anyway."

Nickie looked up in surprise. "You mean you made enough money?"

"I will," said Grover. "I made ninety-seven words out of 'Sparklewash for Dishes.' That ought to be enough to win."

They walked back down the trail together. Grover talked about albino animals most of the way—how rare they were, how he'd never heard of an albino bear before, how some people had considered them sacred in other times and places. Nickie listened with half her attention. A sadness had come over her. She was sad that Grover probably wasn't going to win his contest and go on his expedition, and she was sad that Greenhaven might have a new owner by now, some stranger who wouldn't love it as she did. She felt tired, and sad, and cold.

Overhead, the clouds had gathered and darkened, filling in the whole sky.

"Looks like it's going to snow," said Grover.

CHAPTER 26

Catastrophe

"How was the open house?" Nickie asked.

"Lovely," said Crystal.

"And did anyone want to buy the house?"

"Well, we have an offer," said Crystal. She didn't sound as happy as Nickie thought she would.

"From who?"

"A couple named Hardesty. Retired, children grown. Looking to start a senior health center. Vitamins, herbal remedies, exercise equipment. A library with books about how to cope with hair loss and stiff joints and swollen ankles and that sort of thing." Crystal looked dispirited. "I don't love the idea," she said. "But they offered a good price, and they're ready to sign as soon as they sell their house in the city. I called your mother about it. She thinks we should accept."

So it was over. Goal #1 lost—no hope at all. Once again, that night Nickie crept upstairs after Crystal had gone to sleep and spent the night in the nursery with Otis. He curled up close under her chin. His fur smelled of the woods.

In the morning, Nickie got up while the sky was still dark. She took Otis out, stood with him in the cold while he did what he needed to do, and took him back upstairs. Then she climbed into the bed in her regular room to wait for the light.

As soon as a gray streak showed in the gap between the curtains, Nickie got up and got dressed. She moved quietly. In the chilly kitchen, she made herself some toast and drank a glass of milk. Then she went out to see what was going to happen when Mrs. Beeson's helpers came to get the dogs.

She didn't know when or where the dog pickups would start—but as it turned out, it was easy to find them. As soon as she got down the hill, she saw a school bus moving slowly down Main Street. There were no children in it. At Trillium Street, it turned right. A blue van behind it made the same turn; on the van's side, in white letters, was printed "Church of the Fiery Vision." In the front seat, next to the driver, Nickie saw Mrs. Beeson. Other people were in the van, too. It was full.

Nickie followed the bus, walking fast.

The bus and the van pulled up at a small brown house. Out of the van climbed Mrs. Beeson and several men, including all four of Yonwood's police officers. One of the policemen knocked on the front door of the house.

A man came to the door, leading a medium-sized brown-and-white spaniel. He patted the dog twice and then went quickly back inside and shut the door. The policeman led the dog to the bus and lifted it inside. Everyone got back in the van, and it moved on.

This is how it went—Nickie followed and watched it all. Other people trailed after the bus, too; she saw Martin among them, nodding sternly as he watched the dogs being collected. How could she ever have thought she liked him?

All around her, people commented on what was happening. Most of them had decided, it seemed, that Mrs. Beeson was doing the right thing. "It's hard, of course," said a stout middle-aged woman in a green knit hat. "But doing the right thing just *is* hard sometimes, isn't it? I don't have a dog myself, but if I did, I'd give it up in a heartbeat."

A bald man in round glasses nodded. "I know a lot of people who had trouble with this," he said, "but once they made the decision, they were proud of themselves. They felt *strong*, you know what I mean?"

Nickie thought of how giving up hot chocolate had made her feel: strong, yes, and proud of herself for doing a hard thing. But how could you feel that way about your dog, who was going to be thrown out into the cold? It wasn't just *you* giving something up; you were making the dogs give up their home, and maybe their lives.

The woman in the green hat nodded. "We have to trust in our Prophet and put aside our own selfish feelings," she said. "For the good of all."

But it was hard for Nickie to see the good in what was going on. At each dog-owning household, the bus stopped, the police went to the door, knocked, and then waited while the people inside put the leash on their dog and brought him or her out. Some people put on a brave or saintly face like the first man: they simply patted the dog once or twice on the head and then went back inside and closed the door and did not watch the men lead the dog away. At other houses, there were scenes, especially if children lived there. Loud crying came from inside, and some children even broke away from their parents and ran out and grabbed their dog's collar, screaming, "No, no, you can't take him!" and the policeman had the sad duty of uncurling the fingers from the collar, and the parents had to wrestle the child back inside. A very few families refused to open their doors at all. Mrs. Beeson wrote down their addresses.

After about an hour, when a second and third bus had been added to the first to hold all the dogs, and a chorus of barking, whining, and howling came from the bus windows, Nickie began to tremble, as if she had a hard-beating heart in every part of her body. Her teeth chattered, but not just from the cold. Suddenly she couldn't stand it anymore. She ran, heading back home to get Otis and hide him where no one could find him, just in case, just in *case,* somehow the dog bus came to Greenhaven.

As she ran, she kept saying to herself, It's all right, it's all right, no one knows he's there, I have plenty of time, he's safe, no one knows about him, only Amanda and Grover, so he's all right. But still, the sound of barking and shouting followed her as she ran.

Crystal would probably be there. But Nickie didn't care anymore if Crystal found out about Otis. She'd have to find out soon anyway. It was time for her to know. And Crystal would help her hide him— wouldn't she? She wouldn't let him be taken away.

But when she got to Greenhaven, Crystal's car wasn't there. Where could she have gone? Out to breakfast? It didn't matter. Nickie raced up the path and bounded up the stone steps. She opened the front door and dashed inside and started up the stairs. And stopped short just before reaching the second floor, because there was Amanda, standing at the top of the stairs with Otis in her arms.

Nickie stared—but then relief swept through her. "Oh!" she said. "You thought of it, too!"

Amanda didn't move. "Thought of what?" she said. Otis licked her neck, and she lifted her chin to get away from his tongue.

"To hide Otis," said Nickie. "So they won't find him. Even though nobody knows he's here, it would be better—"

"They do know he's here," said Amanda. She still didn't move.

"Oh, no! They do? Then we have to hurry! How do they know? Come on, let's—"

"I told Mrs. Beeson," said Amanda in a cool, flat voice.

"You what?" Nickie's heart seemed to stop.

"I called her up and told her. Course I did. Did you think I'd want to mess up everything? Did you think I'd go against the Prophet?"

Nickie ran at Amanda and grabbed at Otis with both hands. Amanda pulled him away. "No!" she cried. "She said no dogs! I have to take him!"

"You can't take him!" Nickie reached again for Otis, who was now thrashing wildly in Amanda's grip, but Amanda darted to the side and turned her back, clutching Otis close to her chest, and when Nickie came at her again and grabbed her arm, she made a sudden ferocious twist, sending Nickie staggering across the floor, and turned back toward the stairway. Nickie got her balance and came after her.

When Amanda reached the top of the stairs,

234

Nickie was close behind. She could have pushed her. It would have been easy. Amanda would have dropped Otis, who'd have scrambled away, and she would have fallen down the whole length of those hard, polished steps. She might have broken bones. She might have been killed. The urge to push her was so strong that Nickie just barely kept herself from doing it. Instead she grabbed for Amanda's shirttail, Amanda jerked away, and Nickie fell back and sat down hard on the top step.

Before she could get up, Amanda was halfway down the stairs. Nickie followed, but Amanda was too far ahead. When Nickie reached the bottom step, Amanda was at the front door, throwing it open. When Nickie got to the front door, Amanda was racing down the path toward the sidewalk. And when Nickie made it to the sidewalk, Amanda was running as fast as she could toward the corner of Cloud and Trillium streets, where the blunt yellow nose of the school bus was just coming into view.

That was when the sobs came up in Nickie's throat and the tears flew from her eyes, and she kept running and crying, but only for half a block, because she could see the man coming down from the bus and Amanda running up to him and holding out Otis, and the man taking Otis into the bus. At that point Nickie stood still and screamed. Someone came out of a house and scowled at her. She screamed again. The bus moved on, turning a corner. She ran after it, crying so hard she could scarcely breathe, but it turned another corner and disappeared.

Two desperate urges arose in her: one was to find Amanda and choke her to death, and the other was to find Crystal and make her drive after the school bus, so she could get Otis back.

Finding Otis was more important than choking Amanda. But where was Crystal? Nickie stood in the street looking wildly around, rooted to the spot, trying to think what to do. Maybe Crystal had left her a note. She ran back to Greenhaven and dashed from room to room, but no note was there. Maybe Crystal was at the restaurant. With trembling hands, she fumbled through the phone book and found the number, but when she asked if Crystal was there, the person who answered said no. Finally she ran outside again and stood in the street. Could she run downtown and try to find the school bus and somehow bash her way into it and rescue Otis? She didn't know. She couldn't think. Her breath came in hiccupy sobs, and her heart was running like an engine out of control. She wailed; she couldn't help it—a long, wavery wail.

And at that moment, Crystal's car came around the corner. It drove up the street and pulled in at the curb, and instantly Nickie was beside it, pounding on the window, which Crystal rolled down.

"They've taken Otis!" Nickie cried. "Amanda—she

came—she *betrayed* me and stole Otis and he's in the bus with all the dogs! You have to help! Please, please! If we follow the bus, we could get him—"

Crystal gaped at her. She had a paper cup of coffee in her hand. A white bakery bag was on the seat beside her. "What in the world are you talking about?" she said.

"They're taking the *dogs*!" Nickie cried. "There's no time to explain! Please, please, can you just drive me? And I'll tell you about it while we go."

Nickie's frantic face must have persuaded Crystal. "All right," she said. "Jump in."

CHAPTER 27

The Chase

As fast as she could, in a few short sentences, Nickie told Crystal everything.

Crystal kept interrupting, turning to Nickie with wide eyes and a dropped jaw.

"You mean you've had a *dog* up there all this time?"

"There was a *girl* in the *closet*?"

"You've been *battling* the forces of *evil*?"

"She says dogs are doing *what*?"

But all Nickie wanted was to find out where the buses had gone. "Never mind, never mind," she said. She was still having trouble talking because of breathing so hard and shaking. "I'll tell you later. Go that way." She pointed down Cloud Street. "That's where Amanda gave— But then it turned the corner, I think onto Birch Street—and that was maybe five minutes ago, or ten, so I don't know where the bus is now."

Crystal headed down Cloud Street. "Where did this Prophet woman say they were going to take the dogs?"

"Into the woods, she said. Far away, into the woods where they belong, and then let them go so they can be wild the way they're supposed to be."

"Odd," said Crystal, driving through the neighborhood as fast as possible without actually squealing the tires. "Dogs haven't been wild for several hundred thousand years. Not most dogs, anyway. They need us."

"And we need them!" Nickie wailed. "I need Otis!"

They curved up onto Spruce Street but saw nothing. No one was in the street. A few snowflakes sifted down from the sky and landed on the car's windshield. Crystal put on the wipers. She headed down Grackle Street and turned onto Main Street.

Nickie shouted, "Look!" and pointed ahead. Far down at the other end of Main Street was a patch of bright yellow. "The bus!"

But a moment later it turned off Main Street and was gone.

"It went to the right," said Nickie. "That's High Peak Road; it goes up the mountain. So that means they've finished collecting the dogs, and they're taking them away. Can we go faster?"

Crystal stepped on the gas. "If we *do* catch up to the buses," she said, "what happens next?"

"We just follow them till they stop." Nickie was

leaning forward, both hands gripping the dashboard. "Then when they let the dogs out, we grab Otis."

"What about everybody else's dogs?"

"I don't know. I wish we could save them, too."

"What if the people on the bus refuse to let us have Otis?"

"I don't know, I don't know," said Nickie. "Let's just go really fast."

They turned up High Peak Road. It was a narrow, winding road, with the ranks of trees standing close on either side. The snow was falling faster now, whirling toward them, making it hard to see. Crystal slowed down. There was no sign of the buses.

"I don't know," said Crystal. "This might not be a good idea."

Nickie said nothing. She kept her eyes glued forward, staring through the spinning whiteness. How would Otis survive in a snowstorm? He was little. He didn't know how to get his own food.

Crystal glanced over at her. "Why didn't you tell me about this dog before?"

"I thought you'd take him to the pound. You said you would."

"I did?" Crystal shook her head. "So you've been getting fond of him all this time, haven't you?"

Nickie nodded. Tears came to her eyes again, and she couldn't speak.

"I don't get it," Crystal said. "This Prophet woman

says the love you give a dog is subtracted from the love you give God. Have I got that right?"

Nickie nodded. The sky was growing darker as afternoon turned to evening. The shadows in the woods were so thick she could no longer see between the trees.

"So would that apply to cats, too, I wonder? Parakeets? Hamsters? Undeserving people? How do you decide what's okay to love, according to the Prophet?"

"I don't know," said Nickie. She didn't want to talk about this now. She just wanted Crystal to hurry up. The car was going slowly around the curves. Crystal had turned on the headlights, but they brightened the spiraling snow more than the road ahead. Nickie's neck hurt from craning forward, trying to see.

"Love is love, seems to me," said Crystal. "As long as what you love isn't armed robbery, or bombing airplanes, or kidnapping little children."

"Can we go faster?" Nickie asked.

"Not without sliding off the road." Crystal shook her head. "We're going to have to give this up, I think. It's dangerous." She slowed down even more to go around a bend in the road, and then suddenly she stamped on the brakes and the car slid sideways. Careening toward them out of the blinding whiteness was something big and yellow.

"The bus!" screamed Nickie. "It's coming down!"

Crystal pulled over and stopped. Behind the first bus was another one, and another, each one furred with white on top. They passed by and trundled on downhill.

"But are the dogs still in there?" Nickie said. "Or did they let them out?"

Crystal pulled the car back out onto the road. "My guess is that those bus drivers didn't want to drive in this weather any more than I do. I bet they just dumped the dogs and turned around."

"Then let's keep going!" Nickie cried, bouncing frantically in her seat. "We can find them!"

Crystal drove on, but she was frowning at the road and going slower than ever. After about ten minutes, they came to a place where the trees thinned out, and on the right was an open field, lightly dusted with snow. Nickie could see a dark mush of tire tracks here. "Stop!" she cried. "I think this is where the buses turned around. Can we get out and see?"

"We're turning around, too," said Crystal, but she stopped the car. Nickie flung the door open and jumped out. She ran toward the tire tracks and scanned the field. At the far edge, where the forest resumed, she saw something moving. A dog—no, two dogs, or three—leaping across the snow-dusted ground, heading for the trees.

"Otis!" Nickie shouted, though the dogs she saw

were too big to be Otis. "Otis, Otis, come! Come back!"

But the dogs disappeared into the woods. If they heard her at all, they paid no attention. It was just an adventure to them, a thrilling freedom—at least at first. They didn't understand yet that there were no food bowls in the woods, no warm fires, no people.

Crystal came up and stood beside her.

"I want to go after them," Nickie said. "Will you wait for me? I'll just run across there and call Otis again from where he can hear me—"

"We've got a snowstorm starting up," Crystal said, "and it's almost dark. I can't let you go plunging around in the woods. I'm afraid we're too late."

"No!" cried Nickie. "It's just over there," she said, pointing across the wide field to where the trees made a dark line in the distance. "Otis!" she screamed again.

But nothing moved out in the field, and the snow whirled faster, filling the air, until the trees had vanished behind a blur of white.

"We have to go," said Crystal. Her voice was sad and kind.

All the way back down the mountain, Nickie said hardly a word. She sat staring through the passenger-side window at the tree trunks ghostly in the snow, knowing it was too dark to see anything moving among them, but unable to make her eyes look anywhere else. She felt as if a hundred stones had collected inside her.

Crystal pulled up outside Greenhaven. "I'm sorry about this, sweetie," she said. "I just had no idea any of this was going on. How could I not have known it?"

"You were busy," said Nickie. "With other things." She was so tired all of a sudden. She barely had the strength to open the car door.

But even after they got inside, Crystal kept asking questions, and Nickie kept having to explain things, and then they had to have something to eat, which Nickie wasn't hungry for at all, and Crystal had to talk about how strange it was that no word had come from the president about whether there was going to be war. It seemed like forever before Nickie could get into bed and close her eyes. And of course by then she wasn't sleepy anymore. She lay there thinking about Otis out in the snowstorm, cold and hungry and alone. She thought about the white bear, which might eat small dogs. She thought about Mrs. Beeson, who was trying to do good and was causing so much pain, and about Althea Tower, the Prophet, whose vision had started everything. And she thought about what she herself had done, and at that she buried her face in the pillow and tried not to think at all. "I want my mother," she whispered, "and my father. I want to go home."

CHAPTER 28

One More Trip to the Woods

In the morning, a white cloak of snow lay across the ground. Rooftops and tree branches wore caps of white, and from the bedroom window, Nickie saw that the mountainside had turned from gray to silver. The sun shone down on this white world and made it glitter.

It was beautiful. If she hadn't been so sad, Nickie would have rushed outside to make snow angels and snow caves. But she didn't have the heart for it this morning. Besides, Crystal had plenty of work for her.

Nickie begged Crystal to drive her up High Peak Road again so she could look for Otis. But Crystal said no. This was a busy day. They'd never find the dog—the woods were vast, and besides, everything was buried in snow. And anyhow, they'd be leaving soon, and what would Nickie do with a dog?

Nickie's orders were to clean out the nursery—put

the lamps and furniture back where they came from, pack up the toys and games and other things, throw out anything old and useless. All morning she worked on this. It was awful not having Otis there. When she picked up his food bowl and his water bowl, a lump of sorrow rose into her throat. She put the bowls in a big plastic bag so she wouldn't have to look at them.

She was going to keep the picture of the Siamese twins. Crystal had told her she could have it, either to keep or to sell. She'd called an antique expert and asked about it, and he offered to pay $350 for it, sight unseen. But Nickie wanted to keep it, along with the cross-written letter. After all, these were among the few souvenirs she'd have from this whole trip. She put them carefully at the bottom of her suitcase.

She'd asked Crystal if she could keep her great-grandfather's notebook, too. She felt as if he'd kept her company, a little, while she was here in his house. Now she picked up the notebook and riffled the pages, thinking again about the mystery they contained. The professor had encountered a pool of sadness in the west bedroom, and he had seen something there, too, or thought he had. She sat down on the window seat and flipped through until she found that entry:

1/4 Extraordinary experience last night: Went into the back bedroom to look for the scissors, thought I saw someone in there, over by the bed—dark-haired figure, transparent swirl of skirt. Dreadful feeling of sorrow hit me like a wave. Had to grab the doorknob, almost fell. Figure faded, vanished. Maybe something wrong with my eyes. Or heart.

Reading this again, she remembered something: the long-ago death of a child, and the mother's grief. And the dates: January 4 for the death, January 4 for the echo her great-grandfather had felt. If that's what he'd really felt, an echo.

Could it be? When the child died, the mother would have felt such a knife-like sorrow that it might have left a scar somehow beside the bed in the west bedroom, a scar so deep it could last through a hundred years and more. And the old professor, near death himself, might have felt it, might even have caught the merest glimpse of the grief-stricken mother as she had stood there on that awful day.

Or, thought Nickie, closing the notebook and staring outside at the light on the snow, maybe the professor had read about this tragedy somewhere and forgotten that he knew it. Maybe he'd just imagined what he saw and what he felt. Or maybe he'd made it all up to go with the theories of "parallel worlds" that he was interested in, those "leaks" between the past and present, present and future.

Had he really caught a glimpse of the past? Did the Prophet catch glimpses of the future? There was no way to know.

She put the notebook in her suitcase with the photograph of the twins and the crosshatched letter, and she went back to work on the nursery. When she was finished, the room looked just the way it had when she'd first seen it: empty except for the rolled-up rug and the rocking chair and the iron bed, with a slanted rectangle of sunlight on the wooden floor. What would this room be when the new owners moved in? She hated to think of it filled with dumbbells and stationary bicycles. It wasn't meant to be that kind of room; she just knew it. It wasn't meant to be someone's office, either, full of humming computers and gizmos with little flashing lights. It was meant for children.

After that, she went down to Grover's house to say goodbye. A snowplow had cleared the streets, pushing the snow in lumpy banks to either side. Already, the snow was starting to melt; trickles of water ran down into the street.

Nickie heard bits of conversation as she passed people. Mostly it was about the silence from the White House. No declaration of war. No declaration of peace, either. Just nothing. The nothingness seemed to upset everyone. They argued about what it meant. Good news or bad news?

Nickie couldn't worry about it. Her mind was full of so much else that the question of war seemed far away. She headed down Trillium Street.

No one was sitting on the porch when she got to Grover's house—it was much too cold. She knocked on the door, and Grover's grandmother opened it.

"Hi," Nickie said. "Is Grover here?"

"Down in his snake shack," said Granny Carrie. "They came and took that thing off of him," she added.

"Good," said Nickie.

"That woman has her notions," Granny Carrie said.

Nickie figured she meant Mrs. Beeson. "She wants the town to be perfect," she said.

"In this life," said Granny Carrie, "you don't get to have things perfect. Life is messy, no way around it." She beckoned Nickie into the house, and Nickie went down the hall and out the back door and across the slippery yard to the shed. Inside, Grover was stacking the empty glass cases.

"Hi," said Nickie.

"Hi," he said. For once he didn't make a comic production out of it.

"I came to say goodbye," Nickie said. "We're leaving the day after tomorrow."

"Wish I was," said Grover. He put the cases on a lower shelf and started to spread out some magazines in the empty space. "Did your dog get taken?"

Nickie nodded. She still couldn't talk about it without crying, so she changed the subject. "Did you find out yet if you won any of those contests?"

"Not yet."

"I hope you did."

"I probably didn't. I'll probably be stuck here forever."

"You don't know. Anything could happen."

Grover made a round-eyed, open-mouthed, fake-excited face. "Right!" he said. "All kinds of possibilities! I could get a great job waiting tables at the café! Or I could go be a soldier! Or—oh, boy—the world could blow up!"

"I don't think any of those will happen," Nickie said. Actually, it seemed to her that any of them might; but she could see that Grover was discouraged, and she wanted to cheer him up. "I think you're going to get to go on your trip."

"Hah," said Grover. "You're just saying that to cheer me up."

"No, I'm not," said Nickie, because an idea had hit her, a really good idea, and all at once she was telling the truth. "I can see into the future," she said, "and I *know* it's going to happen."

"Well, fine," said Grover. "And you're going to be president of the world."

Nickie just smiled. "You'll see," she said. "It's been nice knowing you." And she walked back to Greenhaven feeling, for the first time in two days, a little bit good.

The next day the sun shone brightly again. Nickie stood on the sidewalk in front of Greenhaven and watched as a crew of burly men carried one piece after another of heavy, dark, carved-wood furniture down the steps and down the path, grunting and swearing, and heaved the beds and sofas and sideboards into the truck bound for the auction house. She saw the lamp go, the one with the parchment shade. The rocking chair went, too, piled into the back of the truck like a prisoner being carted off to jail. When that truck was full, another one arrived. This time the burly men went down into the basement, where decades' worth of beds and chairs and dining tables were stacked on top of one another. It took hours just to empty out the basement.

When the trucks were finally gone, Nickie and Crystal wandered through the house. Their footsteps thudded hollowly on the bare floors, and their voices, when they called to each other from room to room, shivered with echoes. Strangely enough, though, the house didn't seem sad. Nickie had the feeling it was glad to be emptied out and unburdened. It was taking a deep breath of fresh, cool air, looking out through its clean windows, ready for whatever was coming next. Even Crystal seemed to sense this.

"Really," she said, "it's a fine old place. Without all that ghastly Victorian furniture, it's much improved. You could put, for instance, a white couch right there by the front parlor windows, and a glass-topped coffee table . . ." She held out her arm and tilted her head to one side, imagining it, and then wandered into the dining room. "And then of course a total kitchen remodel. A slate floor would tone in well, and maybe cabinets in birch or white pine to lighten the look. . . ." She stopped in the kitchen doorway, and her arm dropped to her side. "But what am I thinking? It's going to be Senior Haven." She sighed. Nickie sighed, too.

It was sad the way things had turned out. Losing Otis was the worst, but she hadn't achieved a single one of the goals she'd set for herself, either. She wasn't going to live here with her parents after all; she hadn't fallen in love; and she hadn't done a single thing to make the world a better place.

She'd be going away from here next morning, probably forever, so she decided to go up into the woods and look for Otis one more time. And say good-bye to Yonwood.

With the last of her money, she bought herself a snack at the café: a bag of corn chips, two peanut butter cookies, and a bottle of grape juice. She put these in her backpack, along with a small plastic bag full of dog crunchies and Otis's food and water bowls, just in case. She set off up the trail and was soon in the woods, where the sun striped blue tree-trunk shadows across the snow. The sun was warm on her face. She walked with stubborn energy, and every five minutes or so, she stopped and called for Otis. But she heard no distant barking—no sound at all, except for the patter of melting snow dripping from the branches.

She came to the log where she'd sat with Grover three days before. Here she looked out over the view of the town. The sky was deep, deep blue, an upside-down ocean of air. Was God up there somewhere, looking down on the whole world at once? Deciding who was good and who wasn't, figuring out what was normal, planning to sweep everything clean? She wanted to know. She wanted to be sure. But this was one area where her overactive imagination didn't seem to work. She simply could not figure out how a being in the sky, no matter how vast he was, could see everywhere. She didn't see why God would say one thing to the Prophet of Yonwood and another thing to another prophet halfway across the world. Because clearly not all these people who said that God spoke to them heard the same thing. All the fighting nations said God was on their side. How could God be on everyone's side?

Nickie could only think that either there were lots of different Gods all saying different things to different people, or that God didn't really speak to people at all, or that people *thought* they were hearing God speak when really they were hearing something else.

A bird flew across the sky, level with her line of sight. It lit on the top branch of a pine tree, pointed its beak upward, and sang out a long, warbling burble of notes. Did God speak to birds? Or were birds speaking to God?

She called Otis one more time, shouting his name out into the vast air. No answer. Just the bird, singing its heart out. Suddenly she felt finished here. She was ready to go, ready to get out of this place that made her heart hurt. She took off her backpack and got out Otis's bowls. From her water bottle, she filled his water dish. She poured the crunchies into his food bowl. Both of these she set at the side of the trail, next to the end of the fallen log. Maybe he would find them, or maybe one of the other dogs would, and remember its home, and go on down the trail back to its family.

The bag with her snack in it was still in her back-pack. She realized she wasn't hungry. The very thought of food made her stomach clench. So she set the bag on the log. She liked the look of that—a present for a dog, and a present for a person. An offering to whoever might need it. Why not make it even nicer? She walked

a little way off the trail, poking around in the leaf litter, looking up into the branches. Some pinecones lay
beneath a tree, and she picked up the best one, a perfect fat sturdy shape, all its little wooden tabs lined up
in a spiral. She went farther, though in the deep shade
of the pines the snow still covered the ground, and her
shoes sank into it and got wet. She found a bush with
red berries and broke off a branch of it. She found
a smooth, plum-sized stone patterned with veins of
white. She brought these things back to the log and
arranged them around the bag of snacks. The branch
was like an arm around the bag; the berries were jewels. The stone was for her heart, which was heavy
and hard. And the pinecone was just a pinecone—
something nature had made that looked nearly
perfect.

She stepped back and gazed at what she'd done.
Very nice, but it needed a finishing touch. What did
she have that she could add to it? She put her hands in
her pockets and felt around. In her left pocket was a
piece of paper. She pulled it out. It was the picture of
the dust mite, a little bent. She stuck it between the
pinecone and the stone, so that it stood up. It added a
note of strangeness that was exactly right. It seemed to
say, "Remember, I am here, too, along with other
things you can't see. The world is full of endless
strange surprises."

She started back down the trail. If no dogs find the

food, she thought, maybe squirrels will. Or that white bear. Or if no one finds it, then it can all be for God. Only not for the Prophet's God, her mean, picky God who dislikes so many things. It's for *my* God, the god of dogs and snakes and dust mites and albino bears and Siamese twins, the god of stars and starships and other dimensions, the god who loves everyone and who makes everything marvelous.

CHAPTER 29

The Last Day

The next morning, Crystal had a great deal of business with the post office. There were twenty or thirty boxes of stuff she'd decided to save from Greenhaven that had to be shipped back to her house in New Jersey, so much of it that she couldn't fit it all in the car at once. It took her three trips.

While Crystal was at the post office, Nickie roamed around the empty, gleaming house. She went into every room and said goodbye to it—the front parlor, the dining room, the cleaned-up kitchen, the bedrooms, all swept and empty. In the west bedroom, she waited to see if she might feel a trace of the sadness that had washed over her great-grandfather, the grief left there from all those years ago. But all she felt was her own sadness at leaving this house behind.

Finally she went up to the third floor. Here the two trunk rooms were still crammed with the things of the past, waiting for Crystal's decisions. The nursery was empty, but as she stood by the window seat, she could almost feel the presence of the beings she'd encountered there—the letter writers and journal keepers, those who had taken pictures and had their pictures taken, those who had made scrapbooks and saved postcards and lived their lives in this place. And, with an ache, she felt the bouncing, wriggling, eager spirit of Otis.

Down below, the doorbell rang. She was the only one here, so she'd have to answer it. She went downstairs to the front hall, and when she opened the door, there stood Amanda with her suitcase. She looked terrible. Her hair was falling out of its barrettes, her skin was broken out. On her face was the look of someone expecting to be shot in the next three seconds.

"I don't want to talk to you," Nickie said.

"No, you have to let me," said Amanda. Her mouth wrinkled as if she was going to cry. "I have to tell you something."

"*You killed Otis!*" Nickie said. She swung the door hard, but Amanda put her hand out to stop it and took a step in through the doorway.

"But listen," she said, and now she really was starting to cry. "I thought it was right. It was a sacrifice! It was *so hard* to do it, but Mrs. Beeson said the harder the better. If it's real, real hard, you know it's right! That's what she said." She looked imploringly at Nickie, but Nickie glowered at her. "And," Amanda added, "everybody else was givin' up *their* dogs, so I thought it must be right."

Nickie turned her back on Amanda, but she didn't try again to close the door. She went into the front parlor and sat down on the bare floor with her back to the wall beneath the windows. Amanda followed.

"I wish I hadn't-a done it," she said. "I been thinkin' about him all this time, out there in the snow." She actually said "snow-ow-ow," because a sob came up inside the word. She lifted up the hem of her sweater to wipe her nose.

"Well, how come you changed your mind?" Nickie said.

"Because I couldn't stop thinking about Otis," said Amanda, "and because I found Mrs. Beeson's list."

"What list?"

Amanda sat down on the floor facing Nickie. She took off her jacket—the sun was warming the room now—and Nickie saw that she looked thinner than ever. "It was this piece of paper in Althea's kitchen," Amanda said. "A little edge of it stickin' out from under the telephone book. So I looked at it. I shouldn't've. But I did."

"So what was it?" Nickie kept her voice cold and hard so Amanda wouldn't think they were friends. But she was interested.

"Names," said Amanda. "About fifty of 'em. At the

top of the list it said 'Sinners'—just that one word. Then there was names, and by each name a couple words. Like 'Chad Morris, defiant, surly.' And 'Lindabell Truefoot, sluttish.' And 'Morton Wilsnap, queer.' And then 'Amanda Stokes.'"

"You?" Nickie forgot to stay cold and hard, she was so surprised.

"Yeah. And after my name it said, 'disobedient.' How could that be true?" Amanda's voice rose in a wounded wail. "I always did every single thing she told me to do."

"You sure did," said Nickie, going hard again.

"Except for one thing, which was I bought a couple of those romance books I like to read. She found 'em and scolded me. They'd sway me in evil directions, she said."

"What's supposed to happen to the people on this list?" Nickie said.

"Bracelets. It said that at the bottom. They're all supposed to get those bracelets. Even *me!*" Amanda crossed her arms over her thin chest. "Well, I'm not havin' one. I'm leavin' on my own, goin' to my cousin in Tennessee. I don't much like her, but it's better than being here. But I had to come to you first and tell you I'm sorry. About Otis. I wish I hadn't-a done it, I really do."

She looked so miserable that Nickie almost felt

sorry for her. But she thought of Otis out there in the melting snow, his feet wet and cold, his belly empty, and she tried to steel herself against Amanda.

"So do you forgive me?" Amanda said.

"If you could get Otis back, I might," said Nickie.

"But I can't. I'm catchin' a bus in twenty minutes." Amanda actually clasped her hands together and held them up under her chin like someone in an old-fashioned picture. "*Please,*" she said.

And Nickie remembered that she, too, had wanted to do whatever Mrs. Beeson told her, that she, too, had wanted very badly to be right. And also that she'd been just a hair away from pushing Amanda down the stairs. So she looked at Amanda's tear-stained face and hauled up forgiveness out of herself. "All right," she said. "I guess I forgive you." It was a grudging forgiveness but the best she could do.

Amanda sprang up. "Thank you," she said. "I'm goin' now."

"Right now?" said Nickie. "You mean you left the Prophet by herself?"

"It doesn't matter," Amanda said. "They'll find someone else to take care of her."

"But you left her alone? She's alone right now?"

"She is, but it's okay. She's just sleeping." Amanda picked up her suitcase and went to the door. "Bye," she said, and she walked away.

261

Nickie watched as she went down the sidewalk, moving with a sideways tilt because of the suitcases. And as soon as Amanda was out of sight, she threw on her jacket and dashed out the door, heading for the Prophet's house.

CHAPTER 30

Nickie and the Prophet

Nothing was moving around the house on Grackle Street except for a bird that fluttered around the empty feeder and then flew away, disappointed. Nickie tried the front door and found it open. She stepped into the silent house. No one was in the living room, so she went down the hallway, looking into all the rooms. A kitchen. A study. A bathroom. No one was in any of them. At the back of the hall was a flight of stairs, and she went up them. At the top, she found herself facing two doors. She hesitated a moment. Then she chose one of the doors and pushed it open.

She saw a room full of books. Shelves to the ceiling, books on every shelf, and at the end a big soft armchair by a window. Books on the floor, books on a desk. The chilly light coming in through the glass. Outside the window, another empty bird feeder. But no one there.

So she backed out and tried the other door, and when it opened, she saw that she had found the Prophet's room.

What had she expected? A dark den? Something like a church, with holy paintings and statues of angels? It wasn't like either of those. It was an ordinary room, with a bed beside a tall window. The window was closed; the air was stale. In the bed was a woman with ripply light brown hair spread out against a pile of white pillows. Her face was small and pale, and her huge frightened-looking gray eyes seemed to be staring past Nickie, or through her. Her mouth was partly open, but she didn't speak.

Nickie stepped in. Her heart was pounding like a drum. She hadn't thought about what she would say when she saw the Prophet, and now her mind went blank for a moment.

"Ms. Prophet?" she said. "I have to ask you . . . ," she began. The Prophet didn't move. Was she listening to her? Did she even see her? Nickie started again, louder this time. "Ms. Prophet! I'm Nickie! I have to talk to you!"

The Prophet's hands fluttered on the covers, but she said nothing.

So Nickie hurried on. "It's about the dogs," she said. "Why did you say 'No dogs'? I have to know."

The Prophet's eyebrows came together in a puzzled frown, as if she were hearing a foreign language.

She gazed down at her hands. Her lips moved, but no sound came out.

Nickie spoke more loudly. "They took the dogs!" she said. "Did you know it? It was because of you! They took Otis—he's up in the mountains, he's gone—and they took Grover's snakes! Why? I have to know why!"

The Prophet's mouth opened. She looked confused, or afraid. Strands of hair fell across her face, but she didn't brush them aside.

Suddenly Nickie couldn't bear it. All her grief and anger rushed up in her like hot steam, and she took three fast steps toward the Prophet and grabbed her by the arm and shouted right into her face: "Talk! Talk! You have to tell me why they took the dogs! You *have* to!"

At that, the Prophet finally spoke. "Dogs?" she said in a feeble voice. "Dogs?"

"Yes!" cried Nickie, shaking the Prophet's arm. "Mrs. Beeson told us the dogs had to go! She said we shouldn't love dogs, we should love only God. I don't understand it. I want you to explain it!"

For a second the Prophet gazed at her with burning eyes. Then she sank back onto her pillows and went silent again.

Nickie let go of her arm. It was hopeless. Maybe the Prophet's mind had been vaporized by her vision. Maybe she couldn't communicate with human beings anymore, only God.

So Nickie turned away. She went to the window and looked down. There was the backyard where, she'd heard, the Prophet had had her vision. It was such an ordinary backyard—a small brownish lawn, a chair, some trees, a few birds fluttering around. Nickie pushed the window open, and a draft of cool air flowed in, along with a few notes of birdsong. She stood there staring down, breathing the fresh air, feeling sort of empty, like a sack that everything's been spilled out of.

Behind her, the bed creaked.

Nickie spun around. The Prophet was sitting up. Her hair fell over her white nightgown, tangled and long. She pushed her covers away, swung her legs over the side of the bed, and stood next to it, trembling all over. She was hardly taller than Nickie. When she spoke, her voice was soft and raspy, as if she hadn't used it much for a long time, but her words were clear. "I forgot to fill the bird feeders," she said. "When did I last fill them?"

"I don't know," Nickie said. "Months ago."

"Months?" The Prophet passed a hand over her eyes. "How could it be months?"

"It was," said Nickie.

The Prophet just shook her head. "You were saying something to me," she said. "I didn't understand. Tell me again."

So Nickie explained again about how they'd taken the dogs.

"And what else?"

"They stopped the church choir, and radios, and movie musicals, because you said, 'No singing.' It was God's orders, Mrs. Beeson told us."

"God's orders?" said the Prophet.

"Yes," Nickie said. "And you said, 'No lights,' so people turned all the lights off."

The Prophet swept tangles of hair away from her face, stared at the floor, wrapped her arms around herself, and shivered. She stood without speaking, and Nickie thought maybe she had gone back into silence. But abruptly she raised her head again, and this time when she spoke her voice was stronger. "Listen," she said. "I've been ill. I have been ill and heartbroken and drowned in my vision. It's time for me to come back. Will you help me get dressed?"

So Nickie did. She brought clothes from the dresser and the closet, gray pants and a thick white sweater, and she helped the Prophet put them on. When she was dressed, the Prophet sat back down on the edge of her bed, tired. "Explain it again," she said. "Brenda Beeson—what has she been saying?"

Nickie explained again about Mrs. Beeson figuring out what the Prophet meant, and looking for anything that was wrong or evil, and how people were supposed to love only God, not singing or snakes or dogs. . . .

And while she was talking, the Prophet's great gray eyes filled with tears, and the tears rolled down her pale cheeks. "I understand now," she said. "She made a mistake. It was what I was *seeing,* that's what I was talking about. The vision—I couldn't stop seeing it. It was dreadful beyond words. A world burned and ruined. A world with no cities. Everything gone! All gone, all gone."

"You said 'sinnies.' Mrs. Beeson thought you meant 'sinners.' But you meant cities?"

"Yes, yes. The cities all destroyed. People gone. No singing or dancing. No lights. No animals. No dogs, even. All gone! It was what I *saw.* It wasn't orders from God."

Nickie was so astonished that her mouth fell open and she forgot to close it for a second. "It wasn't?" she said when she could find her voice.

The Prophet shook her head. "It was just me."

"Oh!" Nickie stood still, feeling stunned, to let this sink in. She thought of something else. "Why did you say, 'No words, no words'? That was one Mrs. Beeson couldn't figure out."

"No words?" The Prophet put a hand to her forehead. "I don't know. Why would I say that?" She murmured, "No words, no words." Then she looked up, and tears sprang to her eyes again. "Oh!" she cried. "It must have been 'no birds'! *No birds!* Think of a world without birds! It's not bearable." She picked up the nightgown lying next to her and wiped her eyes.

"Maybe your vision wasn't true," Nickie said. She felt sorry for the Prophet, who seemed so frail and sad. She wanted to comfort her. "Maybe it won't happen."

"Maybe not," said the Prophet. "I don't know. I keep having these terrible dreams where my vision starts up all over again. I see the leaders about to begin the war, and I cry out, 'Don't do it!' but they don't hear me." She shuddered.

Nickie came and stood close to her. "I just want to make sure," she said. "You didn't say we shouldn't love dogs?"

"No," said the Prophet. She reached out and took both of Nickie's hands in hers. "Oh, no," she said, softly but very clearly. "No, I would never say that. I love dogs. I love the whole world—all of it." For the first time, she smiled.

"Well, good," Nickie said. "I guess I'll go, then. If you're all right, Ms. Prophet."

"Oh, please," said the Prophet. "Call me Althea. I don't want to be a prophet. And what shall I call you?"

Nickie said her name.

"Thank you, Nickie," said Althea. "I believe you've wakened me up." She stood up rather unsteadily and immediately sat back down again. "Maybe if I got some fresh air," she said.

Nickie walked with her to the window, and Althea took a long, deep breath. "It feels so good," she said. "And listen—birds."

But Nickie was listening to something else. It was a faint sound, off in the distance, but clear. It was the sound of barking.

CHAPTER 31

Love

Nickie's heart gave a huge thump. "Dogs!" she said. "It sounds like dogs! I have to go."

"Yes, yes," said Althea. "Go! I'm so glad you came, but go now—quick!"

Nickie ran down the stairs and outside. The barking was louder, a yipping and yelping, with some ruffs and woofs mixed in, a chorus of dog noise. Where were they?

She ran toward the park. Other people were coming out of their houses, too, shouting to each other. When Nickie got to Main Street, she joined a stream of people. Cars on the street slowed down to see what was happening—and among them, Nickie suddenly saw, was Crystal.

"Crystal!" shouted Nickie. "Stop! Come here!"

Crystal rolled down her window. "What?" she called. "What's going on?"

Nickie just pointed—because at that moment she saw the dogs coming from the uphill end of the road, a jouncing, prancing, jostling gaggle of dogs pouring around the bend and down toward the town, ten dogs or twenty or thirty. She ran toward them, and in just a few seconds the pack was all around her, streaking by, and she turned to race after them. "Otis!" she screamed, trying to make out his small body among the flail of legs and tails. "Otis, where are you?"

They were coming through downtown now, and people burst out of the stores and halted, open-mouthed, on the sidewalks. The dogs ran down the middle of Main Street, and it looked to Nickie, pounding after them, as if they might just run on through the town, out the other side, and back into the woods. But instead they swept around the corner when they came to Grackle Street, raced through the little park, and whirled in a circle, the lead dogs veering around to chase the dogs at the rear, around and around like a tornado, until finally a few dogs broke away, and then more did, until most of them had stopped running and were nosing around the garbage cans or raising their legs against the trees.

By now a crowd of people had rushed down the street to the park. Nickie was among them. Their voices flew all around her. "I see Max!" someone cried joyously, and someone else called out, "Look! There's Missy! Here, girl! Come on!"

Right in front of Nickie, a few people wearing "Don't Do It!" T-shirts halted at the edge of the park. They stood there with their shoulders hunched and arms folded, as if to ward off any dog that might come near. "This is a bad sign," one of them said. The other muttered something that Nickie didn't stop to hear.

She pushed past them. Where in that swirl of dogs was Otis? Was he there? She didn't see him. A boxer had knocked over a garbage can, and five or six dogs rushed to paw through the contents. A black dog was on its hind legs at the drinking fountain, lapping water from the stopped-up bowl. People rushed every which way, calling dogs' names, clutching them by the collar, and the dogs leapt up, licked faces, thrashed tails back and forth.

But where was *her* dog? A dread seized her. What if he wasn't—?

But he was. There, under a picnic table, nose to the ground, sniffing at a scrap of paper, tail pointing straight up. "Otis!" Nickie screamed, and he looked up in surprise. When he saw her, he cocked his head, stared a moment, and then ambled toward her with the scrap of paper sticking to his nose.

She caught him up in her arms, squeezed him tight, rumpled the top of his head, and told him how happy she was over and over. He wiggled. He licked her chin. Twigs and burrs were tangled in his coat, and his feet were wet and packed with mud between the pads.

He smelled like earth and rot and dog doo. He was a mess.

Then a sharp voice rang out above the noise of the crowd. "Wait! Wait!" it cried. "This is wrong! We mustn't do this! We can't take them back!" And Nickie saw Brenda Beeson standing at the edge of the park, wearing her red baseball cap and waving her arms above her head.

A few people turned to look at her; a few of them paused. Then a dark-haired woman bent down, scooped up a small dog, and took it over to Mrs. Beeson. It was Sausage, Nickie saw—with her droopy ears all stuck with burrs.

Mrs. Beeson stared at Sausage. She reached out— and then she pulled her arms back. She turned away, she turned back again, and finally she just stood frozen, with a look of desperate confusion on her face.

And at that moment, a gasp arose from the Grackle Street side of the crowd, and all heads turned. Down the sidewalk, slowly and slightly tippily, came Althea Tower. She was wrapped in a voluminous gray cape, and although she had tried to fasten her hair back with a ribbon, most of it had come loose, and the breeze made it float around her head. She was so short and slight that she looked almost like a child—a frail, excited child, hurrying toward the place where something was happening.

People were so amazed to see her that they just stared as she came closer. At last, two young men ran forward to help her. They led her into the park. People crowded around her, and Nickie heard her say, "Yes, thank you, yes, I'm all right. A girl came and shouted at me—that girl right there"—she pointed at Nickie, smiling—"and, well, I woke up." Then she murmured something to the young man on her left and tilted her head in the direction of Mrs. Beeson. They walked with her to where Mrs. Beeson stood flabbergasted, her eyes darting back and forth between Althea coming toward her and Sausage squirming in the arms of the dark-haired woman. Althea took Mrs. Beeson by the arm, and the two of them went apart from the crowd to talk.

Nickie, who knew what they would be talking about, saw no need to stay any longer. She left the park and the chaos of people and dogs behind and carried Otis back toward Greenhaven. When she was halfway there, Crystal, who had driven home and parked the car, came running toward her. "What in the heck is going on?" she said.

"The dogs are back," said Nickie. "Look. This is Otis."

Crystal stooped over and looked Otis in the face. He opened his long pink mouth and yawned at her.

"Cute," she said.

275

"I'm keeping him," said Nickie.

"I don't know," said Crystal. "Does the building you live in allow—"

"It does," Nickie said, though she didn't know if this was true. She didn't care. She'd make them change the rules if she had to. If they wouldn't, she'd make her mother move.

"Well," said Crystal. "Hmm." But she didn't argue.

Back at Greenhaven, they put the last of their belongings into their suitcases and carried them out to the street. The sun blazed down, glinting off the car and the scraps of snow still left from three days before. They put their suitcases in the trunk. "I have to stop at the real estate office on our way out," Crystal said. "Just for a second."

While Crystal was in there, Nickie sat in the car with Otis on her lap and picked the stickers out of his fur. Dirty as he was, and smelly, she adored the feel of him leaning against her. After a while he got sleepy and lay down with his head hanging sideways over her leg, and she adored the way his mouth looked upside down, with his black lips and the tips of his teeth showing. She picked the dried mud out from between the pads of his feet and didn't mind at all that she got dirt under her fingernails.

Crystal came out of the real estate office quite a while later, just as Nickie was starting to wonder what was taking her so long. Len was with her. When she got into the car, she rolled down the window, and he bent over, curling his hands over the windowsill. "So I'll let you know," he said. "It should be tomorrow or the next day."

Crystal nodded. "I don't even know how to feel about it," she said. "But you'll call me."

"Oh, yes," said Len. He looked at her in a meaningful way. "Oh, yes, I'll call you. Never fear."

Crystal smiled. She put one of her hands over one of his. "Goodbye, then," she said, looking up at him, and quickly he poked his head a bit farther through the window and kissed her on the mouth. It was just a peck, but even Nickie, with her limited experience of being in love, could feel that it was quite thrilling to both of them.

Crystal pushed the Up button to close the window. She put on her sunglasses. She stepped on the gas. They sailed down Main Street and out of Yonwood.

"What's he going to call you about?" Nickie asked as they rounded the curve toward the highway.

"The offer on the house. Looks like the Hardestys are vacillating. They've found another place they think might be better for their purpose. They might withdraw their offer."

"Then what?" said Nickie.

"I'm not sure." Crystal accelerated and merged with

the traffic on the freeway. "It depends on . . . I don't know. We'll see."

They rode in silence for a while. Nickie worked on getting a twig untangled from Otis's ear hairs. Then she said, "Len sure likes you."

A small smile appeared on Crystal's face. "I know," she said. "I like him, too."

"Is he going to come to New Jersey and be your boyfriend?"

"Oh, heavens," said Crystal. "I don't think so." She stepped hard on the accelerator and passed two slow trucks. Still smiling that small smile, she glanced over at Nickie, who was working very slowly on the twig, trying not to pull Otis's hair. "I think you're in love," she said.

Nickie looked up, startled.

"With that pup," said Crystal.

And with a sort of shock, Nickie realized it was true. She had definitely fallen in love with Otis. This *was* being in love, wasn't it? Looking forward to seeing him every day, feeling like a hole was ripped in her heart when he was gone, jumping for joy when he came back, not minding if he smelled bad, wanting to take care of him, actually *liking* the dirty and funny-looking parts of him? Surely it was being in love. It was true that she hadn't fallen in love with Grover, the obvious candidate. She'd fallen in love with a dog instead of a person. But that didn't matter. It was still love. She'd apply it to a person later on.

They drove back to the city. There Nickie carried out the good idea she'd had. With Crystal's help, she sold the photograph of the Siamese twins for $350. She added $25 of her own, and she sent that money to Grover. She put it in an envelope with a note that said, "Congratulations! You have won first prize in the Grand Amalgamated Products Association Sweepstakes!" A few days later, she got a postcard from Grover that said, "A very nice specimen of the Triple-Fanged Magenta-Spotted Rat Snake will soon be on its way to you in the mail. Thank you." Fortunately, no rat snake arrived.

It turned out that their building in the city did *not* allow dogs. But it also turned out that this didn't matter, because of the letter that came from her father the very day Nickie got home. Her mother opened it and gave a joyful shout. "He says his job has been made permanent, and he wants us to come and join him!" she said. "You'll never guess where he is!"

"Oh," said Nickie. "I forgot to tell you. I know where he is—California."

"You're right," her mother said. "But how did you know?"

"He told me, in those postcards," said Nickie. "I

figured it out. I knew he wouldn't be writing those strange P.S.s for no reason."

"They made no sense to me at all," said her mother. "What did they mean?"

"If you'll get the postcards," Nickie said, "I'll show you."

Her mother brought her the postcards, and Nickie laid them on the table. "Look," she said. "It took me a while to get it, but I finally did. Each one of these messages has a number in it. 'Three sparrows.' 'One peanut butter cookie.' 'Midnight'—that's twelve. And 'ninth birthday.' It's the very simplest code—Dad taught it to me. The numbers stand for letters in the alphabet. Three is *C*. One is *A*. Twelve is *L*. Nine is *I*. By the time I got that much, I knew where he was."

"Aren't you clever!" said her mother. "And isn't it wonderful—California!"

"Yes!" Nickie threw an arm around her mother's waist and hugged her. She knew what California meant to her mother, who'd grown up there and whose family had lived there for generations. For her mother, going to California would be going home.

They spent the next week packing, and as they packed Nickie told her mother everything about what had happened in Yonwood—about Otis and Amanda, about the Prophet, about Grover and his snakes, and about the three goals she'd set for herself.

Love

"What happened with those goals?" her mother asked. "Did you reach them?"

"No," said Nickie. "Not really, except for falling in love with Otis. I didn't reach a single one."

But she was wrong about that. Sometimes it takes much longer than you think it will to reach the goals you set for yourself. And sometimes—as it happened with Nickie—you reach your goals in strange and unpredictable ways.

What Happened Afterward

The house in California was on a farm that spread out at the foot of low green hills. There were acres of land for Nickie and Otis to wander in. Nickie loved living there. Snow fell in the winter, and in the summer the fields were full of butterflies.

Crystal went back to New Jersey. Len came to visit her there, and she went to Yonwood sometimes to visit him, and it didn't take long for them to decide they were meant for each other and should get married. Luckily, the Hardestys decided to withdraw their offer on Greenhaven, giving Crystal the chance to make the decision that had been slowly growing in her mind. She took Greenhaven off the market, and she and Len moved into it themselves, filling its rooms with the kind of plushy pale furniture Crystal liked. Four children followed, a girl and three boys, who used the third-floor nursery room for games, puppy training, movie watching, and bouncing on a small trampoline. Two parakeets lived there, and one hamster. For the next five summers, Nickie flew across the country and spent a month at Greenhaven with her small cousins, and in this way she fulfilled, more or less, her first goal.

The summer Nickie was twelve and Grover was fourteen, the two of them paid a visit to Hoyt McCoy, and he showed them the universe that shimmered on the walls of all his downstairs rooms. Then he took them upstairs and showed them his telescope and whole rooms full of astronomical equipment. "I search for signs of extraterrestrial life," he told them. "It's difficult to search in this universe because everything is so far away. Fifty years for light to get here even from the *nearest* star—ridiculous! But other universes—which might be right next to ours, closer than that chair there—that's something else again." His eyes gleamed. "Imagine a rift, a crack in our universe that gives us access to another one. Only for an instant, just long enough to see that it can be done. Would you believe such a thing possible?"

They said they didn't know.

"*I* know," said Hoyt. "Not that I can begin to explain it to you. But that winter you were here, Nicole—well, I will just say that certain people in Washington were astounded by what I told them."

"Washington?" said Grover. "Astounded?"

"Quite. Astounded enough, at a crucial moment,

to put aside certain dire plans. Astounded enough to think that perhaps it was better to explore the world than destroy it. But I am saying too much. Never mind, never mind."

They pestered him with questions, but he would say no more.

Nickie always wondered, after that, if Hoyt McCoy had had something to do with preventing the war. People had waited for over a week after the president's deadline, with nothing but rumors in the news. Finally there came an announcement: an agreement had been reached with the Phalanx Nations after all; war had been averted. No country set off its arsenal of bombs, and the terrorists seemed to fade back into whatever dark corners they had come from. For a while, there were wild rumors that the government had received messages from an alien starship that taught the leaders how to solve their problems. But that was never proven, and hardly anyone believed it. Most people thought that they'd come through all right because God was on their side.

Brenda Beeson was extremely upset to discover that the Prophet's blurry words had not been orders from God. In fact, she couldn't quite believe it. She warned people not to lose faith, and to keep up their battle against evil. She pointed out that although war hadn't come, the terrorist was still up there in the woods. Then one day that spring a young photogra-

pher named Annie Everard took her camera up the trail
to take pictures of wildflowers and came back instead
with a fairly clear shot of a white bear. Everyone was
relieved. Now that the danger was past, they decided to
go back to following regular laws made by people
rather than commands that might or might not come
from God.

Mrs. Beeson found this extraordinarily frustrat-
ing. She ran for mayor the next year, but when she lost,
she took up a life of study instead. She set up an office
in her house, equipped with a powerful computer that
had a lightning-fast Internet connection and all kinds
of software for finding and reading and organizing
information, and there she pored over holy writings
from every place and time, trying to figure out, once
and for all, what God was really saying.

Althea Tower asked everyone *please* not to call her
the Prophet. She was sorry for all the things that had
been done in her name, especially the episode of the
dogs, even though it wasn't her fault. So she set up a
place in her backyard where people could bring their
dogs when they went away on trips. She also led bird-
watching walks around town for anyone who wanted
to come, and she kept her birdbaths and bird feeders
full both winter and summer. She tended to have night-
mares, though, and she never completely recovered her
health.

Grover was in Yonwood only occasionally in those

years. After the Arrowhead Wilderness Reptile Expedition, he spent the next year living with his father's sister in Arizona so he could work with the Young Herpetologists program there on the weekends, and when he was seventeen and had graduated from high school, he went to study in Thailand. His life turned out to be the very one he'd wanted: adventurous, interesting, and useful. He traveled through the swamps of Malaysia, the forests of Kashmir, and the deserts of northern Africa; no one knew more than he did about the strange, endangered creatures of those lands.

Years later, Crystal sent Nickie two newspaper articles from the *Yonwood Daily.* One was about Grover. He had become, the article said, a world-renowned expert on a previously unknown Amazonian snake called the flame-tongued boa. He'd discovered that a gland in its throat produced a chemical that could be used to make a powerful painkiller, and the painkiller was now used by doctors all over the world. When Nickie heard this, she smiled to herself, remembering her Goal #3. On that first trip to Yonwood, she *had* done something to help the world after all: she had started Grover on the road to his discovery.

The other article was about Althea Tower. It was simply a brief notice of her death. She had caught a bad flu that developed into pneumonia, and she'd died at the age of sixty-four.

And so the Prophet wasn't around when it began

to look as if her terrible vision might be coming true after all.

The problem was, the conflicts that threatened the world when Nickie was eleven had never really been resolved. For a while, leaders turned to the quest for knowledge, putting their efforts into finding out what secrets the universe might hold, and the world changed in many ways. But time passed, the leaders of one era were succeeded by the leaders of the next, and the old fears and differences arose again, fiercer than ever.

And so, long after Nickie had grown up and married and had children, after her children were grown and gone, after her husband (who'd fulfilled her Goal #2) had died—that was when the world once again plummeted down toward darkness. Perhaps, Nickie thought, the Prophet really *had* seen a glimpse of the future—just a more distant future than anyone had thought. What was happening certainly matched the horrors that had frightened her so badly.

All over the world, people who believed in one truth fought against people who believed in a different truth, all of them believing theirs was the only *real* truth, and all of them willing to do anything—absolutely anything—to defend it. Nations readied and aimed their missiles. They sent their soldiers to take over cities and fight for land, and as the fighting swarmed across deserts and jungles and seas, new diseases broke out, and warring troops and fleeing refugees carried them to one country after another; hundreds of thousands died. Fear ran like a pack of wolves across the planet, and people were afraid for the survival of the human race.

That was when the enormous project that Nickie's father had worked on fifty years before was at last put to use. It was an entire city, built beneath the ground, stocked with supplies and sealed off from the surface so that its inhabitants could live there as long as necessary, safe from whatever was going to happen above. When the human race seemed truly threatened, the government contacted a few carefully selected people and asked if they might be willing to volunteer for this enterprise. Nickie, being the daughter of one of the Builders, was among them.

She was torn. She hesitated a long time before making up her mind. She loved the world and didn't like the prospect of going down into a dark place and remaining there, probably, for the rest of her life. But *because* she loved the world, she finally decided to go. She was sixty years old, after all; she'd had many good years of life. But she wanted to make sure people were still around after she was gone to keep on loving the world. Who would appreciate its beauty and wonders and strangeness if people were gone? So she volunteered. And as she sent off her letter of acceptance, she remembered again her long-ago Goal #3: to do something good for the world. She'd tried her best to help the world during her life, doing the small things that came along. Maybe this was a big thing for her to do— the biggest, and the last.

Besides, she was curious. What would it be like to live in an underground city?

When the day came, she was both sad and excited. On the train, she began keeping a journal, but when the travelers got to the cave entrance and had gone down a long tunnel to the river that would take them to the city, she was afraid the leader would catch her writing (it was against the rules), so she wrapped her journal in a green plastic rain hat, wound a narrow belt around it a couple of times to hold the plastic on, and stashed it behind a rock. Maybe someone will find it someday, she thought. It will be a sort of letter to the future.

Will anyone find Nickie's journal?
What will the world be like
when they do?

Read the rest of the story in
<u>The City of Ember</u> and
<u>The People of Sparks</u>.

Acknowledgments

My thanks to all those who helped and encouraged me through the many drafts of this book, including Susie Mader, Pat Carr, Charlotte Muse, Patrick Daly, Sara Jenkins, Molly Tyson, and Christine Baker. Special thanks to my editor, Jim Thomas, for pushing me relentlessly when I most needed pushing, and also to Jordan Benjamin, for sharing his expert knowledge of snakes (including a live demonstration of snake dinnertime).

Jeanne DuPrau is the bestselling author of *The City of Ember* and *The People of Sparks*. She has been a teacher, an editor, and a writer of nonfiction. She's always wanted to live in a huge, mysterious old house with secret passages and ghosts, but for now she lives in a rather ordinary house in California, where she keeps a big garden and a small dog.